I0452979

NAIMA:
A TERRAMATES NOVEL

LISA LACE

NAIMA
Copyright © 2016 Toppings Publishing.
All rights reserved.

Disclaimer

This book is licensed for your personal enjoyment only.

Copyright Notes

No part of this publication may be used or reproduced in any form or by any means, including printing, photocopying, or otherwise, without written permission from the author, except in the case of brief quotations embodied in critical articles or review.

If you would like to use material from the book (other than just simply for reviewing the book), prior permission must be obtained by contacting the author at lisa@lisalace.com.

CONTENTS

CHAPTER 1

GABRIELLA

I had finished my day at work, and it was time to relax at home. Yoga would clear my mind. I tucked my legs underneath me, breathing out deeply. As my eyelids closed, I propped my back against the wall.

Trying to stop thinking about everything racing through my head was always a mission, almost like a second job. I owed a lot of money. I didn't want to dwell on it, but it was always at the back of my mind. It was going to take *forever* to pay off all my debts. Sometimes the neutral hum of my desktop computer could soothe my mind and lead me directly to sleep, but not tonight.

I would have to do other things to relax. I tried to focus on the rising and falling of my chest, feeling my body begin to loosen with each breath I took. I imagined a peaceful scene. The picturesque stretch of Two Moons Lake materialized in my mind. I saw a wooden dinghy floating on the glittering green water. The view never failed to pacify my turbulent emotions. I liked to imagine it was my private island, a perfect, unperturbed space for me and my thoughts to run free.

My mind descended into peace. All I felt was the easy, cottony comfort of my sweat pants.

Ding.

My eyes popped open, moving to the new message alert flashing on my desktop screen. I hoped something good had broken my meditation. I kicked out my legs with an irritated sigh and hopped to my feet. Once I got close enough to read the sender's name, my eyes turned into slits. My stomach churned, and I felt the bitter sensation of resentment. I didn't want to see that name ever again, but there it was.

Jake Turner.

At one point in my life, that name would have meant the world to me. The very thought of Jake once left my knees weak. I was different back then; I was a silly, love-struck sixteen-year-old, and I latched onto the first "real" man who showered me with any amount of attention.

Jake was twenty-three, he had a car, and he was sexy as sin. Those tattoos, piercings, and the irresistible dimples on either side of his pearly-white grin were overwhelming. Jake was a stereotypical bad boy, and I had to get my hands him.

Looking back I could recognize that the attributes which attracted me to Jake were both superficial and negative, but at the time, they were *exciting*. On the eve of my seventeenth birthday, I emptied my room. I stuffed all my clothes, plastic jewelry, and anything that ever meant something to me into two duffel bags. I carefully snuck out of my house and into the dead of the night. Jake's clunky secondhand convertible seemed like a horse-drawn carriage to me, waiting to whisk us off to my happily ever after.

Guess how long that lasted?

My bubble of delusion popped in a few weeks. Living life with an unemployed boyfriend whose primary objective in life was to sit on his couch and try to kill people in Call of Duty wasn't as glamorous as you might think. I convinced myself he was still young and conflicted, and assumed Jake's aimlessness was a symptom of him trying to navigate his way through life.

Picking up the slack for the both of us, I started juggling two jobs and eighty-hour work weeks. Jake only got off his ass when it was time to do odd jobs with his friends in painting or construction. Money ran through his fingers. I know he went on drinking binges and late-night parties with his friend, but he never contributed to the rent or our stack of bills.

I'm not sure why I stayed with him as long as I did. What I did know was that going back home with my tail tucked between my legs wasn't an option for me. I was going to make the most of what I had. I had a roof over my head, and I wasn't living on the streets. I had even grown accustomed to our predictable routine. From an outsider's perspective, you would think we were friends with benefits, not lovers. Maybe not even that - he was more of a couch surfer. But his name was on the lease.

A couple of years later, my hands and arms were covered with raw callouses, oil spatters, and bleach burns. Jake was usually passed out on the couch in a booze-induced coma. I was a minimum wage zombie clocking in and out of work. I decided to make an effort to get a better job. If my relationship with Jake wasn't getting any better, maybe the problem was our finances. Unfortunately, I didn't have a high-school diploma, but I worked with what I had.

I talked my way into a full-time job at an upscale boutique. As a junior sales associate, my wages were low, but I kept my mouth shut and worked hard. I went through every position in the store before I made manager. It felt like heaven. I would get year-end bonuses, additional time off, and a raise. Everything was going to change for us now. I knew a fresh start was just around the corner.

One lazy Tuesday afternoon, I left the assistant manager in charge and headed home early to surprise Jake. Before I could kick off my shoes by the front door, I was greeted by the sight of Jake fucking two trollops on my living room couch. I couldn't get over the betrayal. The threesome was the final strike against Jake.

I experienced an unnerving feeling of déjà vu when I packed up everything I owned. Undeterred by Jake's blubbering apologies, I crammed everything I bought with my salary (which was everything in the apartment) into boxes and suitcases…even the game console I bought him last Christmas.

My eyes had stared at the desktop monitor for so long that they were beginning to water. The mouse wavered between the *Read* and *Dismiss* buttons of the message alert window. Time to make a decision. I sucked in my breath and tapped *Read*.

itz_big: Hey babe. U holding up without me?

itz_big: It's been 3 months. You ready to stop this tantrum and come home yet?

Disgusting. I knew he couldn't see me, but I pretended he could. I crossed my arms, cocking my head to one side as I thought about the brazen, shameless stupidity of his words. Whatever else you might think about Jake, he apparently had balls of steel. Thinking back about all his mistakes took me into a furious rage.

I had been late to work countless times because I was tending to a twenty-something loser who couldn't handle his booze. I spent many nights alone while he was out frolicking with his equally juvenile friends, drinking God-knows-what and screwing God-knows-who. The worst memory was finding him balls-deep in a silicone Barbie doll, whose lusty screams continued to haunt my nightmares.

Maybe that was the second worst memory. The worst memory was discovering Jake had stolen my identity and used it to open a bunch of credit cards under my name. The money disappeared a long time ago, but I was stuck paying the bills. Even though I received a pay raise as manager, I was going to be working for a long time to climb out of debt.

Ok. *Dismiss*. Click. Done. My computer beeped softly, clearing the message from my screen. I returned to my bed and tried to meditate and clear my mind. Even though my eyes were squeezed tightly shut, my heavy breathing and racing mind stopped me from achieving any inner peace.

Ding.

Fuck. I couldn't believe it was Jake again. I opened my eyes and dragged myself to my feet, but the computer monitor was still dark.

This time, it was my phone notifying me I had a message. With a frown, I picked it up and checked the screen. The message was from a new app I had installed yesterday. It was called M8r, from the TerraMates company.

The message wasn't from **itz_big**. The username was **GenLaz241**. I thought about accepting the request.

TerraMates specialized in marrying Earth women with aliens. Sounds ridiculous, right? But at this point, I had given up on having a fairy-tale ending for my life with a human man. All the same, I thought there was someone out there for me. Maybe my special someone just wasn't on this planet.

I had never felt like I belonged on Earth. It sounds silly, but these thoughts were in my mind since I was a child. Humans are inherently selfish, and nothing ever changes. We participate in an endless cycle of war, poverty, and heartbreak. The same news stories which appear in the headlines today could be topics of conversation from centuries ago. Humanity feeds on endless drama. We refuse to take a step back and learn from our mistakes.

My kindred spirit, my 'Mr. Right,' my soul mate, whatever you want to call it...I knew my special someone is out there. If I had a chance to cross through outer space to fill the gaping hole in my life, so be it.

I usually wasn't one to participate in matchmaking of any kind. In fact, I used to poke fun at people who did. But right now, I was ready to roll the dice and broaden my selection pool. In fact, it was possible to look all over the galaxy. I could wipe my slate clean and find love all at the same time.

What could go wrong?

Before I made my decision, I opened M8r to look up 'GenLaz241'.

Location: Planet Maztek. Languages: Standard, Maztekki, Hindirin.

My eyes bulged when I saw the name of the planet. Dad had been a doctor and humanitarian. He regularly visited Maztek to aid the native population there, kind of like Doctors Without Borders, but the borders were *really* far away. In his down time, Dad promoted relations between Maztek and Earth. He took a lot of heat from his friends for being friendly to aliens, but he always said it was worth it.

Whenever he came back from the planet, he brought me toys and stories about what an enchanting, mystical paradise Maztek was. The best present he ever gave me was a special Maztek lullaby he sang to me when I had problems sleeping.

Dad promised to take me to see Maztek when I was ten years old. He said I would be old enough then. Dad broke the promise when his passenger shuttle crashed. He didn't make it back home in time for my tenth birthday. In fact, he never made it home at all.

Swallowing, I accepted the message request. My phone's screen split. On one side was an image of myself, and I suddenly realized I did not look my best. Shit. I had swept my strawberry-blonde hair way from my face in a sloppy ponytail. The dark rings under my eyes were prominent under the poor light conditions in the room. I fumbled for the lamp and hastily switched it on. My face looked brighter. I tried holding the phone at different angles, wondering if I would look more beautiful from another perspective. Pulling off my scrunchie, I shook my hair loose and fluffed it to add volume.

The other side of screen remained blank.

"Hello? Anyone there?"

"I'm here."

"GenLaz241?"

"The name's Lazarus, but Laz will do."

His rugged voice was husky, with a manly timbre to his curt replies.

"My name is Gabriella Stein. Is your camera working? I can't see anything from your side."

Laz's picture started breaking up. I wondered if there was poor wireless connectivity on Maztek. When it came back, my phone showed a dark room with only a few dim yellow

11

bulbs. In spite of the heavy shadows cloaking his upper body, I could still make out strikingly magnetic features on his face. Forgetting he could see me, I ran a tongue over my cracking lips.

To start with, he was undeniably sexy. He had rich, dark brown waves of hair tied back into a man-bun. A thick beard lined his square jaw line. He had tattoos on his arms. They covered his massive biceps which bulged out under the sleeves of his shirt. I didn't know what the symbols said because they were in Maztekki, but I'm sure they were something profound.

He also looked dangerous. There was something about his eyes that said *Don't Cross Me.* I was sure he had killed before and would kill again.

He leaned closer to the screen. "You still there? I think the camera on your end is frozen." His steely green eyes seemed to look at me through space, and I woke up from my daze.

I tucked a strand of hair behind my ear. "I'm sorry. I've never done this before, not even with a human man. I was overwhelmed."

He growled. "Me too."

Suddenly I felt jittery and started babbling. "A man of few words, huh? I manage a boutique. I would love to do something out of my comfort zone. I'm always up for a good adventure. I love anything drenched in white chocolate. Shit. I'm starting to sound like a dating profile. I'm just nervous, if you can't tell already."

"Don't be."

I shifted in my seat, the shaky grin on my face fading fast as an awkward silence enveloped us.

"What kinds of things do you like?" I asked lamely.

"Excuse me."

With his chin resting on his fist, he peered over his shoulder. He called out in Maztekki, exchanging words with a muffled voice in the background. My eyes focused to his fist, where I saw four asterisks tattooed on his knuckles. My heart skipped a beat.

Without warning, Laz started singing. An alien was serenading me over the phone.

Beyond the four stars, with the whispers of this melody

I carry this heart forever, my naima, you'll be.

The two lines of the lullaby Dad used to sing to me began to loop on repeat in my mind. For years, I had tried to recall the rest of the lyrics to the broken song, but for some reason, those two lines were the only ones that stuck with me all these years. Astounded, I gripped my armrests. I rocked back in my seat, my tongue sliding over the back of my teeth nervously. As he turned back to face me, I held my breath in anticipation.

"Sorry. I'm needed elsewhere. We'll have to cut this short, but we'll talk again soon."

"Oh, but I – right. Okay." Weaving my fingers through my hair, I flashed him a quick smile. "It was nice meeting you, Laz."

"And you, Gabriella."

The phone went black while I was still waving.

Well, that could have gone better. Shaking my head, I slid the scrunchie off my wrist and twisted my hair back. I had been out of the dating field for so long that my social skills were in dire need of a brush-up. I wondered if aliens could tell when Earth girls had problems talking with them.

Ding.

My phone lit up again. *GabriellaS, GenLaz241 has chosen you as his mate. The offer is 500,000 credits. Accept or decline?*

Was this really happening? That was enough money to pay off everything I owed. I snatched up the end of my ponytail, playing with my hair, the bristles pricking at my fingertips. I couldn't think.

I felt like this couldn't be real. I looked at my phone again.

Accept or decline?

It wasn't a difficult decision, but I felt like someone else was in control of my body. I moved my finger forward and pressed accept.

TerraMates was my ticket to a fresh start in life, and there was no way in hell I was going to let it slip through my fingers.

CHAPTER 2

GABRIELLA

Tugging on the lapels of my coat, I stepped onto the steel boardwalk leading to the TerraMates ship. The spaceship was a giant passenger shuttle accented with gold paint and docked at the end of the spaceport. Dozens of families gathered on the landing by the shuttle gate. The other well-dressed women, more mail-order brides I assumed, wore their most fashionable attire. I saw skimpy dresses and elegant ensembles which flaunted their figures. Streaming tears stained their rouge cheeks and painted lips as they hugged their loved ones goodbye.

With a sheepish smile, I lugged my suitcases behind me and slipped past the loving families. I had never felt more out of place or more alone. As I strode past the gaggle, a few of the brides regarded me with raised eyebrows and curious stares.

"You take care of yourself, sweetie – you hear me?" A small family of three grabbed my attention. A pretty bride with a bright, round face and a gorgeous head of black, kinky curls huddled with her mother and father. She placed her forehead against her mother's, carefully touching the elderly woman's face with her thumbs. The bride wasn't crying at all, but her clenched lips and the pained look in her eyes revealed her distress. Her father, a tall and big-boned man, easily towered over his wife and daughter. He ran his fingers through their hair and pulled them close to him. His eyes fell shut, and his lips began to move rapidly in silent prayer.

I realized I was staring at the family. I moved my gaze down to my spiked, four-inch boots. I was becoming overwhelmed with a terrible feeling of nostalgia. After all these years, I should have gotten used to Dad not being around anymore.

For as long as I could remember, I have had the utterly useless ability to maintain eye contact with people speaking to me but hear absolutely nothing at all. I like to think of it as having a mind with a penchant for roaming. Dad used to say I was a shining star, and I shone the brightest when I shut out the world.

I needed to keep out the world so I wouldn't remember how lonely I was.

For the most part, being by myself didn't bother me much, except when everyone else's parents were around. When I saw other dads everywhere, it emphasized his absence. At my first sports game when I was twelve years old, I remember all the other fathers cheering for their children scattered across the field. Dad wasn't there, but I always imagined he would be front and center. If he were there, he would have been the proudest of all the other dads. His hoots, whistles, and cheers reigned above all the rest, and Dad's cobalt-blue eyes glistened with joy...in my dreams.

Dad lived on in my imagination until I was fifteen. When I waved back at my imaginary Dad taking pictures of me from the front row during a choir performance, it piqued the interest of Michi.

"Gabby?"

"What, Michi?" I recalled, snapping at her. I hated it when people shortened my name. Dad gave it to me. It was the only thing of Dad's I had left.

"You realize there's no one there, right? Who are you waving at? Freak."

Michi said this in a cruel stage whisper just loud enough for all the other choir members to hear. I was mortified, not only because of her words, but also because of the mean and uncomfortable laughter around me. I never let my guard slip again. The wishful sightings of Dad swiftly receded.

I had a prepared answer for the few people who approached me, asking where my parents were. I informed any nosy people that they had both passed on.

My mother wasn't dead yet, but she might as well be, for all the love she showed me. Not that I gave a damn. A couple of weeks ago, I had spotted her in the grocery store when I was out running errands. I had hidden before we crossed paths. Lurking behind a concrete wall, I watched her with a peculiar mix of disgust and pity. It had been less than ten years since I saw her last, but it looked like she had aged twenty. I wondered if she had a drug problem.

Her sagging gray skin was pock-marked. She used to have rich, luxurious brown hair. Now her hair was thinning, revealing bald patches of her pink scalp. She was also twice the size I remembered. She was a wheezing, panting mess, struggling to balance the groceries in her arms with her bulky frame.

Standing idly by, watching the woman who gave birth to me struggle to feed herself might seem heartless to some. In retrospect, I guess it was cruel. Unfortunately, I had never experienced kindness from her. She was nothing like my dad. My mother was everything I never wanted to be – nasty, shallow, superficial, and above all, weak.

After Dad died, my mother rapidly married again, attaching herself to a new man named Richard. I suppose she might have loved him. To me, he would always be the prick she slept around with behind my father's back. Richard appeared in our house in a matter of weeks. It felt as if my mother let the drunk bastard move in before I could even shed a tear for Dad.

From the very beginning, I knew there was something wrong with Richard. He acted as if he owned our place immediately. He was rude, cocky, and obnoxious. My mother made sure to keep her new man happy but didn't pay any attention to her flesh-and-blood. I stood aside and watched as Richard and Mom squandered all the money Dad saved for us.

At least they spent it on healthy things, like fast food and liquor. I had to learn to fend for myself at a young age, feeding myself with their leftovers. Other times, I scrambled together bland concoctions from the old food I found around the kitchen.

My 'guardians' made it clear that my exceptional performance at school meant nothing to them. I had nothing to offer them they wanted, and I stopped trying to please them. I realized that I had to live my life for myself.

If you asked me why Richard had it in for me, however, I had no idea.

Most days, I did my best to stay out of his way. He started hitting the bottle regularly around the time my teen angst reached its apex. We seriously started butting heads when I approached the age of fifteen. Unable to keep my mouth shut any longer, I started talking back to him. Each insult I threw in his direction was more daring than the last.

The first time he got physical with me, I learned he wasn't fucking around. As I stepped in to defend my cowering mother against his never-ending battery, he hit me straight in the eye with his fist. Stumbling back to the floor with my vision clouded with stars, the one hundred eight pound man over twenty years my senior kicked me twice in the jaw for good measure.

He would get his hands on me on four other occasions before I finally gathered the courage to leave with Jake. In twisted hindsight, I suppose I should thank the tragic figures in my life for shaping me into the woman I was today.

It didn't matter anymore. My string of bad luck would end here and now.

"Attention, all passengers. This is the final boarding call for shuttle Alpha-912, bound for Maztek. The captain will close the doors in approximately three minutes."

I tightened my grip around the handles of my suitcase and raced toward the gate.

* * * *

The wheels of a beverage cart rolled along tracks built into the floor of the aisle, stopping next to me. "Care for some coffee or tea?"

The shuttle attendant was a well-groomed older gentleman in a cream jumpsuit and immaculate zero-gravity boots that looked functional but had the unfortunate design decision of being bright pink. A loopy quiff sitting on top of his head bounced as he maneuvered his container of supplies. He flourished a hand over the neat rows of mixed nuts, cookies, and chips lining the top of the cart.

He must have seen my face because he quickly offered another product. "Are you hungry for some treats, perhaps?" he said with a smile. "It's been a long flight already, and I'm afraid Maztek is still another three hours away."

I didn't feel like purchasing anything, but he looked so eager that I couldn't refuse. "Just some tea, thanks. I'll have the mixed fruit flavor."

The attendant handed me a silver goblet filled with a fragrant, sweet tea. I sipped from my glass and set it down on a coaster. The back of my head slumped against the cushion of my headrest. I rolled my shoulders and tried to relax. Maybe the complimentary sleep mask would help. I eased the silky blindfold over my eyes.

The problem was that I wasn't alone. Even in the dark, I could still hear the chatter of all the other mail-order brides around me. Maybe they had interesting stories to tell. I could accept a lack of sleep if it meant I would be able to hear amusing snippets of conversation.

"It took ages for TerraMates to verify my profile, but I'm happy they did. I say it's worth the wait. My new husband is a big-time ambassador on Maztek."

"Mine is a second cousin of King Jacquim. He's practically royalty."

I rolled my eyes. What a gold-digger. I had heard her disgusting sugary-sweet voice throughout my trip, and I was already getting sick of listening to it.

"Ooh, Vanessa. You're a lucky girl."

"I know, I *am* lucky! Trinity? Are you still crying about your family? For crying out loud, babe, get over it. You know there's such a thing as a video call in space, right? It's practically free, too. Do yourself a favor, make a call, and quit whining."

Trinity wouldn't give up. "But I —"

"Look at the bright side. Your whole family came out to see you off. It's a shame that some brides have burned all their bridges and are fleeing the planet, coming here by themselves." There was a pause in the conversation. "One wonders what she might have done and why she's running away. I've certainly never seen anything like it."

Was she talking about me? The conversation wasn't amusing at all. It was time to take action. "Excuse me." I slid the sleep mask to the top of my head. "I don't mean to be rude – not that you would know anything about manners – but would you mind keeping it down? A few of us care about our appearance and are trying to get some rest before we meet our mates. It's a long interplanetary journey. We don't need to know every detail of your life and your voice is making the flight feel longer."

I must have been tired, because I sounded rude, even to my ears. Most of the women agreed with me, nodding agreement in the background.

I turned my head to look at Vanessa. She looked gross. Makeup caked her face, and it was impossible to tell what she looked like underneath. Still, now that I saw her, she looked strikingly familiar. Did I know her from somewhere? I thought she might be good-looking underneath the makeup, but a permanent sneer ruined her appearance. My eyes widened in recognition. I remembered where I had seen her before.

Vanessa had seen my epiphany. As she tossed her fiery, pin-straight locks over her shoulders, a fleeting look of panic passed over her face. She quickly recovered, unpleasantly puckering her shiny brown lips. "I can do whatever I want on this spaceship. I know my rights. If you don't like what you hear, don't listen to me. It's as simple as that."

"My apologies." I wasn't sorry at all. Batting my eyelashes innocently, I snunk back into my seat and folded my arms across my chest. "While we're discussing things that aren't anyone else's business, I think I have something to bring to the table. Have you been here before? I suppose the third time's the charm. Am I right, Ms. Greer?"

Vanessa gulped audibly, the color draining from her formerly smug face. She hadn't thought anyone would recognize her. When I was searching online for information on TerraMates, the name Vanessa Greer cropped up multiple times. TerraMates took pride in a low divorce rate. Vanessa had broken so many marriage contracts that she might have been single-handedly responsible for most of the TerraMates failures.

The only reason she seemed comfortable here was because she had already done this twice before. On both occasions, her husbands from the planets Dynotek and Mercury-II were so fed up with her laziness and overall piss-poor attitude that they sent her back to Earth. She was making a bundle. I didn't know how she kept scamming TerraMates, but she had a good con and was working it while it lasted.

Vanessa stopped speaking and stiffly slid down into her seat. The loud gossip quickly died down as the women started using their indoor voices. A victorious smile swept across my lips. As I stretched my arms out, cracking my knuckles, another bride took the seat next to me.

"Thanks for saying something. I was dying for her to shut her trap."

My face lit up. It was the bride I spied by the shuttle gate before boarding. Up close I could see her eyes were hazel. She held her hand out to me, and I accepted it, smiling warmly.

"My name's Cheyenne."

"Gabriella."

"Listen, Gabriella," said Cheyenne. Her face became serious for a moment. "I hope you didn't let her words affect you. She's insecure. You can tell by her attitude. Women like her are trying to get a rise out of anyone. It's a defense mechanism they use when they feel threatened."

"Believe me, I know," I agreed, nodding my head. "I saw you with your folks earlier. Your parents look like nice people. You have a sweet family."

"They are," said Cheyenne wistfully. She hung her head low. "It's going to be tough when I'm away. I can't imagine what my life is going to be like without them, but at the same time, I think it's for the best. My new husband seems nice enough, although my mom thinks I'm rushing into things. We were only talking for six months before we decided on a contract."

"Six months? You mean like half a year?" I echoed weakly.

"I know!" Cheyenne's face became bright red. "It does seem a little rash, doesn't it?" Cheyenne mumbled. "How long did you know your husband before you accepted his proposal?"

Ten seconds? "Uh, about that..."

"What the hell is this?" Our heads swiveled in Vanessa's direction.

"I asked for your oldest wine, and what do you give me? This tastes *disgusting*! Was this fermented from alien shit?"

Vanessa snarled. She hurled the bottle at the attendant's head, who stepped aside as it flew past him. "You're lucky I'm feeling forgiving today..."

Vanessa's diatribe cut short as a thunderous, earth-shaking force struck the spaceship, shaking the floor beneath our feet. I didn't know what it was. Meteorite? Missile? Who would want to shoot a ship full of human females? The incident was short and sweet, but the violent chaos that erupted after the collision seemed to drag on forever.

I thought there was some disaster training before the vessel departed Earth, but I didn't pay attention to it. I was focused on meeting my sexy new alien husband. Now the cabin was full of the blood-curling shrieks of women and crew who saw their lives flashing before their eyes. I looked around for my new best friend, Cheyenne. I didn't want to die alone.

The overhead lights started flickering, and I saw the fear on Cheyenne's face presented in snapshots. Her hand reached out to mine and our clammy fingers intertwined. Some other passengers had paid attention to their pre-flight instructions and we emulated them, moving forward and bracing our bodies for impact.

I could feel a change in the way the shuttle was moving. We were going down. We must have been near a planet and gotten caught in its gravity well. The enormous, spinning hunk of metal was free-falling through the air. I was lucky to be strapped into my seat - the contents of my stomach started shifting as we helplessly let gravity have its way with our ship. I had the urge to vomit, but I was moving around so much I didn't even get the chance. I closed my eyes.

Before I knew it, we hit the surface of the planet. The shuttle bounced along the ground before colliding into a large boulder, settling backward as its motion stopped.

As soon as we hit the ground I had the urge to unbuckle myself and get away to safety. My eyes fluttered open slowly. My eyelids felt heavy, and my vision blurred with tears. I could hear and smell clouds of hissing smoke filling the air around me. Cheyenne's groans added even more to my unease.

But Cheyenne wasn't the first thing I saw. As soon as my eyes focused on something, I realized I should have kept them closed. Vanessa wouldn't have the opportunity to scam TerraMates again. Her body was only inches away from my nose. Her collarbone stuck out from her neck at an odd angle, and her empty, glassy eyes stared me straight in the face.

Before I had a chance to react, a blinding light shined into my face.

"You're coming with me, human."

CHAPTER 3

LAZ

I rolled over on my side. My pillow crumpled under the weight of my head. I was awake, but my pounding head and dry throat kept me from the physical act of actually getting out of bed. One of the privates had fiddled with the camp's particular heating system. As a result, my bunker was stiflingly hot and infested with flying pests.

I expected incidents like this. Most of the privates were morons.

My arms and calves were still sore from doing drills with the freshmen recruits. Despite my clear schedule tomorrow morning, I could not drift back to sleep no matter how hard I tried. I typically subsisted on four hours of sleep, so I was restless.

A magfly flitted past my ear. It found a landing spot on my head and clung onto my earlobe. As I raised an open hand to swat it off my ear, I heard the groan of a sinking floorboard. I sat upright and swung my legs off the cot.

My feet sunk straight into the worn insoles of my boots. I yanked on the pull-chain next to my cot. The lights switched on, filling the bunker with a pale yellow glow. I looked around the room. The file cabinets next to my desk were still intact, and the screen of my desktop was blank. I glanced to the left. The supply closet was bolted shut. My hand-held laser pistols were laid out on my nightstand where I had left them. I did a quick mental inventory of all the rifles hung on the wall.

A slow creak sounded on my right. I suddenly noticed the front door was ajar and lightly swinging back and forth. I wasn't alone. I squared my shoulders and tentatively crossed the room. The door clicked as I pushed it back into place. That was my mistake.

The next thing I knew, someone pulled a foul-smelling sack over my head. With my vision impaired and my oxygen supply threatened, my training only allowed me one course of action. I started swinging blindly at my attackers. I heard a loud crash. Was that the front door being kicked open? Footsteps stampeded in my direction, and my arms were pinned behind my back. Multiple hands knocked me off my feet. My body became suspended horizontally. I couldn't fight any longer as my assailants started carrying me away. Further struggling at this point would be futile. I needed to reserve my energy for later.

Although my vision was impaired, it only heightened my other senses. From the fresh chill brushing against my arms, I knew we were behind the bunkers storing our tanks and shuttlecraft. The noise of boots crushing gravel was so crisp that it sounded as if someone was grinding herbs by my ear.

They lowered my body to the ground so I was able to walk, but surrounded me so I could barely move. I marched forward cautiously, feeling a light poke on my right leg with every step. The frosty blade of a knife strapped to my ankle was my last chance of escape. If I could get to it, I would be home free.

My kidnappers guided me into the back seat of a shuttlecraft. Until now, they had yet to slip up. They hadn't even spoken a single word. I supposed they were communicating with hand signals. Even though I was in a sitting position, I found it difficult to move my arms. Two massive bodies boxed me in on either side.

The ground rumbled beneath my feet. I felt my body being pushed back as the shuttle lifted off the ground. The sack over my head made my nose itch, but I couldn't scratch it. I sat perfectly still for the duration of the ride.

The first noise I heard was two beeps from the spaceship, indicating that we were beginning to descend. As the wheels of the craft deployed and we started rolling on the bumpy ground, I flexed my muscles. My legs clenched and I raised my heels off the floor. If an opportunity presented itself, I would be ready.

I felt a breeze of fresh air as the door of the craft opened. My assailants ushered me towards the exit. But as I leaned forward in the doorway, I felt the beefy fingers around my arms loosen. Taking advantage of the moment, I fished out the knife from my ankle strap and lunged ahead. I collided into several of the attackers. Rolling out of the doorway, I yanked the sack over my head and tossed it aside, looking around wildly with my fist gripped around the handle of my seven-inch knife.

"Whoa! Stand down! General – it's us!"

Although it was nighttime, it was still bright. My eyes were used to looking at the inside of a hood. I blinked away the flashing spots inhibiting my vision. As my sight returned, I saw seven figures around me wearing the same gray army fatigues as myself. I lowered my weapon and raised my eyebrows, bewildered. One by one, the best of my front line infantrymen rose from the ground, rubbing their heads and rolling their necks.

"What the hell is going on here?" I demanded, sliding my knife back into place.

"I told you fools this was a bad idea. Surprise?"

Sergeant Major Dallas, my right-hand man, stuck his neck out of the shuttlecraft. The Zagwog refugee loomed over the rest of the crew, retracting a pair of white wings into his back. His eyes became narrow, which only made his ice-white irises brighter in the dark of the night. Gnarled dreadlocks swung around his face as he shook his head. He strode toward me and handed me my coat. I slipped it over my black tank top and turned to look at the four-story building behind me.

Booming, fast-paced music leaked out of the joint's closed doors. Wealthy men in striped mintchilla coats, ape-skin hats, and platinum chains around their necks filed into the entrance. On the rooftop, colorful spotlights projected onto the skies. I read the sign over the door.

"Jewels?" I mused, frowning. "A strip club? Did you boneheads drag me out of bed for *this*?"

"It's a gentleman's club," Kraig corrected. The Command Systems Operator grinned, running a hand through the spiky strip of hair in the center of his shaved head. "We're all gentlemen, right? We thought we could surprise you. Now that you're tied down, we figured we'd throw you the bachelor party you never had."

"Trust me, General," Maxwell, the Artillery Gunner, piped up. "I'm in here at least twice a week getting the VIP treatment. The girls here are unbelievable. They have the finest tits in town. I swear it on my Mama's grave."

"I don't mean to be a buzz kill, but I'm not in the mood."

"Come on, General," Maxwell pleaded. The other crewmen cried out with shared sentiments. "In all my years of service, I don't think you've ever been to a victory party. Not even the one after we busted the terrorists at Palace Square two years ago."

"All right, all right. One drink," I conceded. Sighing, I fell to the back of the line as the eager soldiers paraded into the club.

"King Jacquim and Princess Ayala send their blessings," said Dallas, walking next to me. "He booked us a private room, complete with bottomless drinks at the wet bar."

"He didn't have to do that. Thanks for planning all of this. I appreciate it."

"It's our pleasure, brother. I know this isn't normally your scene, but I'm sure you'll find a way to make it through this torture."

The club was thick with scented mists and pink fog. There was a long phallic-shaped stage in the middle of the room. A voluptuous Maztek woman with bright orange hair suggestively pressed her back against the pole. Her nipples peeked out from the top of her tiny green bikini. With one hand clasped onto the pole, she cupped her other hand around the side of her breast. She massaged her cleavage, exploring the curves of her body to the intense beat of the song playing overhead. As she danced, the hungry men around her repeatedly threw credits in her direction.

We headed for more illicit pleasure. I followed my men to the back of the seedy establishment. Save for a quizzical few, most of the clientele had their eyes glued onstage and paid no attention to the party of guffawing soldiers. I nodded at the pretty-faced cocktail waitresses staring at us. A blushing waitress wiggled her red eyebrows at me as she held open the door to our VIP room. I winked at her, thanking her softly as I shut the door behind me.

The private suite had a tenfold increase in sterility and swank. A fully-stocked bar sat next to the plush, velvet couches. Three soundproof rooms were cordoned off behind red curtains. A dressed table filled with a bounty of roasted meat platters, sabertooth hog sandwiches, and desserts was pushed up against the wall. As a pudgy bartender entered the room and shuffled behind the bar, my men attacked the table of food head-on and started talking immediately.

"Hey, General! Try one of the bluebird drumsticks. They're juicier than that orange-haired stripper's tits."

"Nice. Do you kiss your mother with that mouth?" I replied, suppressing a grin. I grabbed a skewer and headed for the bar. "I need a drink. You kids have fun."

A few minutes later, six women entered the room. A sketchy individual with the brim of his hat pulled over his eyes followed suit. He carried various sound equipment under his arms. As the man set up his music booth, the women began pairing off with my boys.

A cute stripper with a short, triangular haircut and rows of hoops on both her ears squeezed into the gap next to me. Her short silver skirt barely covered her round ass cheeks. I tried to keep my eyes facing forward, but the tempting line of her bouncy cleavage was distracting.

"General Lazarus?"

"Can I help you?"

"No, but I *know* I can help you," she whispered sultrily. She wrapped her slender fingers around my wrist. "Why don't you come with me?"

"I'm flattered, but no thanks. Why don't you go ahead and take Maxwell?"

"No can do, sir!" Maxwell interjected, sounding smothered. He pulled away from a pair of oiled breasts,

33

taking a breather from his motorboating. His stripper squealed gleefully. "I'm a little busy here! Go on, sir. You'll be in good hands with Trixie."

"Come on, General. I promise I won't bite."

I allowed Trixie to lead me away as my men whooped in the background. We headed into one of the sequestered rooms. The VIP room for VIPs, I supposed. She gently pulled me until I was sitting on the edge of the only chair. Trixie called out a command, dimming the lights and firing up the sound system at the same time. The trippy bass line of a sizzling instrumental started to play softly. She said something else and a single spotlight turned on, illuminating the floor in front of me. Swallowing, I rested my palms on the armrests.

Trixie positioned herself under the spotlight. She lowered her glistening eyes as a coy smile spread on her violet lips. Slowly, Trixie relaxed her body, swaying her hips. Running her fingers across the top of her dress, she pulled it down slightly, showing me a glimpse of her ample cleavage. Her natural brown skin looked smooth, and I wanted to touch it.

She kicked off her heels one at a time, whirling around slowly to make sure I could see every part of her body. With her ass jutting forward, she dipped her head between her legs. The hem of her skirt was raised midway, exposing a black thong wedged between her meaty cheeks. I gritted my teeth, fighting the carnal urge to reach out and give them a good spanking.

Knowing she had my full attention, Trixie wiggled her ass. She stood up straight and bit down on her lip. Her eyes locked on mine. As she glanced back at me, she lifted an open palm and smacked herself hard. It was like she could read my mind. The clothing around my crotch tightened at the sound of the hard slap. I felt movement between my legs when I saw the light pink flush across her quivering ass cheeks.

"Can I tell you a secret, General?" She turned back to face me as she slowly unzipped her dress on the side.

"By all means," I croaked.

"I love dancing for a man in uniform."

I spread my legs, settling against the back of my chair for the first time. Trixie's dress dropped to the floor, gathering around her ankles. She was wearing a complicated web of latex lingerie and looked stunning. I felt like I was losing control of my eyes as they ate up every inch of her hot little body. Two black strips barely covered her nipples, which highlighted the immense size of her tits. Two crisscrossing layers of cloth covered her cute snatch, revealing the vibrant dye on her trimmed pubes around the edges.

She reached to the side for a tube of perfumed oil and unscrewed the top. Drizzling the thick amber liquid onto her body, she rubbed the oil over her arms and legs. She started fondling her breasts with her slick fingers, easing the latex strips off her nipples. Her nipples were perkier than I had pictured them. By now, my cock was fully erect. Its tip prodded against the crotch of my pants.

Trixie danced around me, placing her chin on my shoulder. She hooked her arms around my neck, sliding her hands down my chest. Undoing the front of my jacket, she leaned in and whispered in my ear.

"Do you know what I find hotter than a man in uniform? When the guy isn't aware of how unbelievably sexy he is."

She slipped one hand under my black tank top, feeling the grooves of my stomach. As my shoulders tensed up, sweat started to form on the back of my neck. She began to fumble with the waistband of my pants. My heart drummed against my chest. I could feel her warm fingers inching lower and lower.

As she dragged her hot tongue behind my ear, my eyes glanced at the floor-length mirror across from me. It was like watching myself star in a porn video. For a split second, I considered yielding to my base instincts, and letting myself sit back while she played with my engorged cock. I watched as she unlaced the bow on her hip. The moist strips over her pussy began to loosen.

It was too much. "That's enough, Trixie," I announced gruffly, awkwardly rising from the chair.

"Where are you going? I'm just getting started here."

Buckling up the front of my coat, I extracted a folded bill from one of my pockets and left the tip on the chair. I headed toward the exit, clinging to one side of the curtain like it was a shield. Taking note of the disappointed sigh behind me, I turned back to Trixie.

"It's not you. You're beautiful. Have a good night."

When I left, I made sure the curtain was closed again so Trixie could get redressed.

"That was quick!" Maxwell boomed from across the room. "You know you can have Trixie for another twenty-five minutes, right?"

"I bet he didn't even finish. The General's bride isn't here yet, but she's already got him whipped. Must be some broad, huh, sir?" Jarrod, our Sniper Scout, joked.

I shrugged at my men, double-tapping my elbow at them. I needed a drink. I exchanged pleasantries with the bartender and ordered a bitter ale. The bartender slid a frosted mug of fizzy, dark green liquor across the counter. As I caught it smoothly with my right hand, Dallas appeared at my right side.

"Pay them no mind, Laz." Dallas leaned his elbows against the counter and took a swig from his glass. "They're just messing around. There's nothing wrong with wanting to settle down. It gets lonely out here."

"I hear that."

"Tell me about this girl, Gabriella. Do you really think she's your naima? A *human*?"

My shoulders rose up defensively at the mention of the word. I looked around me to make sure the rest of the men were out of earshot. I would never allow the other subordinates to cross the barrier into my personal life, and I didn't want to appear weak. Even though I would die before admitting it, I was in search of my naima like everyone else. I didn't know if she was Gabriella or not.

At this point, I had made my peace with the fact that I could potentially never find my naima. I didn't know what had compelled me to place a bid on her in the first place. All I knew was that I needed to see her again. It felt right.

"You never know. There's a first time for everything, right?"

My words trailed off as I glanced at the screen on the wall. The game of Krog-ball was interrupted by an emergency news broadcast. Flashing headlines scrolled under the solemn-faced reporter.

"This just in. Under Synic's command, the Xylox army has shot down shuttle Alpha-912, transporting brides from Earth to Maztek. Eight human brides and ten crew member perished in the crash. Xylo soldiers have taken control of the site of the accident. They are holding the remaining brides and crew members as hostages."

The news station switched to a crude live-action feed from planet Xylox. I set my drink on the counter and squinted at the screen. Unfortunate, but none of my concern. The monitor panned to a shot of the brides marching into the Xylo military base.

When I saw the humans, I realized this incident would affect me. Gabriella was the third to last in line. It looked like she had tried to style her blonde hair but it was currently unruly. Her clothing was muddy and torn. She looked scared. I was relieved to see she was unharmed, but at the same time, I felt my gut wrench with a spike of fear.

"Assemble the men," I instructed Dallas. "We're headed to Xylox."

CHAPTER 4

GABRIELLA

I cracked my eyes open one at a time. I was lying on the ground and my nose itched. As I tried to move my hand to scratch the tip of my nose, I realized my arms were stuck. I looked down at my body, feel a sense of dread overcome me. Heavy chrome handcuffs restrained both my wrists and ankles.

My extremities were falling asleep. How long had they bound me like this? I whimpered, attempting to wriggle my ankles, but I got an unpleasant surprise. When I moved, blue bolts of electricity sparked from the handcuffs. A sharp jolt stung the bare flesh of my arms and legs. Shit. I guess I wasn't going anywhere soon. The electric shocks weren't the only thing causing me pain; my entire body was sore, riddled with painful sensations through my back and limbs.

There were bars all around me. I was locked in one of many full-sized cages filling the vast space of a dungeon. It didn't hurt too much when I turned my head. Looking around, I saw other brides from the ship imprisoned just like me, one to a cage. Some were shivering uncontrollably. Others cried. A few whispered prayers into the dark. Blue fluorescent lights illuminated the room, which made the rusted industrial bars of our cages appear sinister.

I was petrified. I wanted nothing more than to raise my voice and cry for help, but the gloominess of my surroundings and the aches in my body sucked up all of my remaining energy.

Where was my friend? "Cheyenne?" I whispered. My voice surprised me. It was trembling and squeaky. Speaking the two syllables made me realize my throat was burning too. The beverage cart on the TerraMates shuttle was far away. I closed my chapped lips. I wouldn't be able to drink a cold glass of water any time soon.

I heard a voice on my right croak out my name. As it turned out, Cheyenne was in the cage next to me. Her formerly springy curls were now frizzy and disheveled, erupting from her head at crazy angles. Her glazed eyes looked swollen and puffy. I was certain she had been crying for hours before I regained consciousness. She seemed to be in shock and stared straight ahead. If it weren't for her heaving chest, she wouldn't be moving at all.

"Cheyenne, are you okay?"

She turned toward me. Fresh tears started streaming down her face. One clung to the base of her quivering chin. Her nose had been rubbed raw, and streaks of red marred her cheeks. Although her emotional condition looked terrible, there were no signs of physical damage other than some scrapes on her neck and elbows.

"Are you hurt?"

She shook her head slowly.

I felt like I needed to say something to cheer her up. "Hang in there. It's going to be okay."

A harrowing scream pierced through the eerie quiet of the room.

"It's not going to be okay. It's Synic again," breathed Cheyenne.

"Huh?" I whispered. "Who's that?"

Before I could get a response from Cheyenne, my question answered itself. I saw a flicker of motion and my eyes moved toward the far left of the cages across from me. An imposing figure wearing a crimson full-body cloak led a group of eight guards toward the cluster of cells. The leader's matching red mask was a frightening visual. It had tinted yellow goggles in the eye sockets, and a large hooked beak that covered his face and nose.

I wondered if the mask helped him breathe or if it was supposed to enhance his appearance. I hoped he needed the mask for medical reasons because I didn't want to know what his natural face looked like, if his mask was that ugly.

The alien guards following Synic looked just as terrifying. Their facial features and builds were humanoid, but the back of their bald heads had swelled up to twice normal size. On the back of their ugly deformed heads was a disgusting pouch that I couldn't help observing. Pink and blue veins covered their heads. Their skin looked dull and white, as if they had never seen sunlight. They dressed better than Synic, wearing color-coordinated black and maroon combat attire. The guards were also well-trained, moving in unison.

Synic raised a leather gloved hand in front of him, spreading his fingers wide. A rattling cage door violently opened in response to his unseen command. Synic curled his fingers into a fist and yanked it back. The shuttle attendant in the pink zero-gravity boots lurched forward, crumpling to the ground by Synic's feet.

What the fuck? Was this guy using the Force or did he have super-science at his disposal?

The attendant's poofy hairstyle was now matted flat against his shiny forehead. Though dried blood covered his battered face, it looked as if he hadn't shed a single tear. I guess he was more of a man than he appeared on the surface. Even though his hands and legs were restrained just like mine, he slowly lifted himself to his knees. One of his shoulders was dislocated and hung limply at his side. I rooted for him silently, watching in horrified awe as the attendant kneeled on the ground.

"Are we ready to start talking now?"

The nonchalance in Synic's words made me uncomfortable. His crackling, metallic voice reverberated across the dungeon.

The attendant didn't look up, keeping his eyes focused on the dusty, cracked floor. The guard on his right raised the butt of a rifle and smashed it into the side of the attendant's face. A loud, nauseating crack ripped across the room. The attendant keeled over, crying out in agony. Even

LISA LACE

though I couldn't see Synic's face, I imagined a slow, vicious grin creeping across his lips.

Synic lowered himself until he was at the attendant's eye level and grabbed the man's chin in his hand. The poor attendant's bruised face looked lopsided from the blow. I winced, unable to imagine his unbearable pain.

"Would you like to try again?"

"Up yours."

The attendant leaned close to Synic and spat in his face. A bloody tooth bounced off his steel mask. Satisfied with himself, the attendant pulled back.

I was astonished that Synic barely reacted. He calmly wiped the spit from his mask with the back of his sleeve and rose to his feet. Synic motioned to his guards. At a flick of their commander's wrist, four sprung into action. Two mindless musclemen stood on the attendant's legs and held his hands behind his back. The other two dropped to his sides. One held the attendant's trembling head in place while the other pried open his jaws.

"I think you must have mistaken my patience for kindness. I will dispose of you like a worthless piece of Earth garbage if you don't tell me the information I'm seeking."

"Never."

The attendant smiled bitterly. His gurgling voice oozed hatred. Synic took a step forward. He pinched his fingers

44

and drew them back slowly. The attendant gagged as his tongue rolled out of his mouth.

"Very well. I suppose you won't be needing your tongue if you're not interested in talking."

I thrust my wrists forward, my fingers wrapping around the cold bars of my cage. Bile rose in my throat. Synic reached inside his cloak and pulled out a knife.

I would never forget the guttural howls of pain that echoed through the room. At that moment, the brides were all silent, pale-faced, and scared to breathe.

Against my better judgment, I opened my eyes slowly, wanting to look at the gruesome scene. Synic blocked the attendant from my view. He wielded his weapon, swiping his blade from left to right. As Cheyenne mourned soundlessly next to me, Synic stepped aside to admire his handiwork.

Blood gushed out of the straight red slit that appeared on the attendant's neck. He gasped for air desperately. Bubbles formed at the opening in his throat. I watched the life slowly drain from his eyes. His body keeled over, landing on the ground with a soft thud.

I hadn't realized my mouth was hanging open. I wanted to go home. The needlessly cruel death sparked a memory in my mind.

I could never find out any information about Dad's shuttle crash. Could these same assholes be responsible for shooting down his passenger craft? If that was the case, and I was retracing his footsteps, I wholeheartedly hoped he died instantly. I didn't want to imagine Dad dying at the hands of these savages.

"Why did you do that, you fucking monster?" Was that me talking?

"Gabriella, no!" Cheyenne whispered urgently.

Cheyenne's voice snapped me out of my daze, but it was too late for me to stay unnoticed. Synic's tinted lenses flashed in my direction. He casually trampled over the attendant's dead body, the back of his cloak dragging against the floor as he approached me. The guards showed their rotten, black teeth and pointed their weapons in my direction. The pointlessness of speaking hit home. I shied away from all the aliens and flattened myself against the back of my cage.

Synic's hand hovered over the lock of my cage. The heavy chains around the door fell to the ground by themselves. The padlock clicked, and the door to my cage screeched open. I felt the soles of my feet float off the ground. My body somersaulted as an invisible force pulled me forward. I crashed hard onto the ground on all fours.

"Please don't hurt her!" begged Cheyenne. *Be quiet!* I silently cried.

Ignoring Cheyenne's pleas, the guards hauled me to my feet. The sharp beak of Synic's mask was unnervingly close to my nose. I closed my eyes, hoping that if I couldn't see him, the situation would resolve itself. It didn't help. I felt like the penetrative eyes of his mask could see right through me and read my thoughts.

"What did you say to me, Earth whore?"

"I – I –"

An earsplitting explosion went off on the left of the dungeon. In place of the wall, there was now a massive hole. Plumes of gray smoke rose from the unexpected explosion. Concrete and steel debris covered the floor. A squad of soldiers burst through the crevice, dressed in identical gray uniforms and military-issued gas masks.

Synic released me at once, charging toward the intruders. I fell back on the floor. I couldn't stop myself from moaning in relief. My movement was restricted, and I could only watch the scene unfold around me.

The masked fighters split into two groups. Half of them battled Synic's guards and kept them at bay. The others wielded laser-edged cutting tools. They snipped open the padlocks and chains on all the cages, freeing the hostages. I crawled back toward my cage, clearing a path for our rescuers.

Synic's guards toppled to the ground one at a time. Sensing imminent danger, Synic moved away from the chaos and vanished. I growled under my breath, but I could only watch as they got away.

"Gabriella! Help!"

One of the intruders had scooped up Cheyenne and flung her over his back. She flailed her arms and legs, wiggling her fingers as she reached out to me. I tried hobbling after her, but my legs weren't working properly. It was hard to move.

"Cheyenne!"

My voice was cut off when a soldier grabbed hold of me and draped me over his shoulder.

"Who are you? Where the hell are you taking me?"

The soldier didn't even acknowledge me. Instead, he moved toward his entry point and kept his weapon aimed in front of him.

We spilled out of a dark maze of tunnels, emerging into open air. The planet looked dead. Overhead was a gloomy gray sky and around me was barren foliage. The soldier took off away from the cages. I peered over my shoulder, marveling at the enormous military-grade space shuttle parked in front of us.

"What is going on? Please answer me!"

I didn't want to find myself in a worse situation. Fed up, I pressed my fingers underneath the edge of his mask and flipped it off his head. I saw dark waves of brown hair pulled back into a man-bun. Sweat drenched his bronzed skin and beard.

I had only seen him once before, but I immediately knew who it was. I couldn't believe it.

"Laz?"

There was no time for him to reply. I watched a missile soar over his head, headed straight for the military shuttle. The missile hit its target.

Roaring flames and suffocating black smoke engulfed the shuttle. A wave of force pulsed through the earth, sweeping us off our feet and hurtling us through the air.

CHAPTER 5

LAZ

We were fucked.

A dull buzz rang in my head as I staggered off the ground. Chunks of burnt metal and seat upholstery covered the dirt around me. Some of the seats were still ablaze. I dusted off the dirt from my clothes and looked around for Gabriella. She wasn't on her feet yet, but she was still alive.

I took a quick head count of my men. They were slowly getting to their feet, appearing dazed but otherwise unhurt. I hadn't been the only one to carry out one of the Earth women; we had tried to save as many as we could. A few of the brides were unconscious. My men picked up the women who were incapacitated and carried them over their shoulders, heading into the woods where they could find cover.

A few Xylo guards still surrounded us. I signaled to Dallas, Kraig, and Maxwell, who pulled out their firearms and created a hail of laser fire, making the Xylo flee. They ushered the remaining brides to safety.

They left the Xylo prick who had destroyed my favorite shuttlecraft for me. I didn't need anyone endangering the lives of Gabriella or my men. The bumbling bastard was still struggling with a missile launcher. He was dragging it along with him when he caught me looking at him. He ditched the shell launcher, which was still leaking smoke from its ashen mouth. I didn't want to chase him down. I pulled out my weapon and shot him twice in the head.

Gabriella started coughing violently behind me. I turned away from the guard's twitching body to face her. She clapped a hand over her mouth and fanned at her face. The black smoke and fumes made her eyes red. One of the sleeves of her dress had ripped and was falling off her shoulder. Apart from the bruises on her arms and legs, she looked like she would survive.

I adjusted the satchel on my back, searching through the wreckage for my gas mask, which had somehow detached from my face in the explosion. Pushing aside several pieces of rubble, I located the mask lodged under a broken headrest. I jogged back to Gabriella and carefully placed it on her head before lifting her off the ground. As she whirled around, swinging her arms behind me, I removed a rag from my satchel and tied it over my mouth.

"Thank goodness I can breathe again, but I can't see anything now! Laz? Are you still there?"

I wanted to respond, but I couldn't say much with a rag in my mouth. Instead, I put my hands on her waist and positioned her behind me, trying to shield her with my body.

My eyes flickered to the region where we had created an entry point in the Xylo outpost. A steady stream of black and red Xylo uniforms moved toward us. In fact, they were coming quickly and appeared to be well-armed. We needed to leave before they overtook us.

Gabriella had seen them as well. "Heaven have mercy..." she muttered. She began to back away slowly.

I pulled my makeshift mask down for a moment. "We're going to have to run for it. Keep your head down and don't look back!" I hollered over my shoulder.

I positioned my weapons on my hips and moved backward. The doomed Xylo in the front absorbed the initial volley. Most of them crashed to the ground. The ones who survived started to panic, shakily raising their weapons. The guards in the back tripped over their fallen comrades, tumbling over in quick succession. I glanced over my shoulder, moving toward the sounds of Gabriella's slow-moving footsteps.

I quickly caught up with Gabriella. Hooking my arm under her legs, I tossed her over my shoulder once again. With my brows furrowed in concentration, I raced up a dismal trail and dove into a dark wooded region. I opened a mirror attached to the rear sight of my weapon and checked behind me. I only slowed down when I was satisfied we had lost our pursuers.

"Damn it! I said, let me down!"

Gabriella banged her fists against my shoulders. Granting her wish, I gently placed her on the ground. I massaged my shoulders and stretched out my arms repeatedly, trying to crack the soreness out of my back. The human woman was heavier than I had anticipated. She alternated crossing and uncrossing her arms, shifting her weight from one leg to the other. With the oversized gas mask over her petite frame, she looked like a giant magfly sizing me up for a bite to eat.

"Is everyone on this planet out of their minds? First, my shuttle gets shot down. Then I get taken hostage by those psycho aliens. When you come along, you start throwing me around like a beanbag. What are you even doing here?"

I raised a hand, indicating that she should hold that thought. When I reached into my pocket, I realized why my men hadn't contacted me. My hand emerged from my pocket holding fragmented pieces of my communicator. The damn thing must have broken when the shuttle explosion tossed me through the air.

I narrowed my eyes and carefully examined the parts of the device up close. Although it was in fragments, I thought I could repair it, given tools and time. The problem was the damaged Morse board. I would have to get a new one if I wanted to fix it.

"Son of a bitch."

My angry words echoed through the stale air around us. I growled, pocketing the useless parts of my communicator. What were we going to do now? I looked around me, trying to analyze my surroundings.

"Laz? What's wrong?" Gabriella demanded. She removed her mask and held it against her hip. "It's like I'm talking to a wall here. I swear, I'd have a more productive chat with my reflection!"

"Put your mask back on," I snapped at Gabriella impatiently, still facing away from her. "Stand down. Let me think."

My nostrils flared as I started to pace. I unconsciously adjusted the knot on the rag, tightening its hold on my face. Even with the makeshift mask, I made sure to breathe out of my mouth. Centuries of chemical warfare had turned the air of Xylox poisonous and chemical-ridden. In the worst parts of the planet, breathing the toxic air could cause severe respiratory problems. Native Xylo developed an immunity to the fumes but were becoming disfigured over every generation.

The uneven terrain barely concealed caves of varying sizes. Although I knew there were animals here, moss and disturbing patches of fungi were the only visible sources of life. All the trees in our spot of the woods looked like they had died a long time ago. Their trunks were thin and sickly, and the few that had managed to stay alive had black, moldy fruit hanging off their gray leaves.

I needed to figure out a way to communicate with my crew so we could all get out of here alive. We only had the supplies and ammunition we carried and it was starting to get dark. I didn't know much about this planet; Xylox was the furthest thing from a tourist attraction.

Mapping out the land would have been my first objective, but all the tracking tools I relied on had been stored on the shuttle. I would have to go back to the roots of my training.

"Laz! Will you please say something before I lose my mind over here?"

I usually worked with military men, and wasn't used to being in a combat situation with a civilian. **"I said, stand down!"** I roared.

Gabriella tripped over her own feet, toppling backward. The look of terror in her beautiful blue eyes made me calm down at once. She had to bite her lip to keep it from trembling. I sucked in my breath roughly and relaxed my stiff shoulders. I took a few steps back to give us both some room.

I felt like scum. Up until now, I had been subconsciously treating her like a soldier under my command. The situation was complex. I suspected that if I tried to put myself in her shoes, I would also be woefully unprepared and want to talk about everything. This was likely her first brush with death or violence, and probably the worst day of her life.

So now what? Should I pat her on the head or something? I had never been comfortable sharing my feelings or talking. I was a man of action.

As Gabriella started to push herself off the ground, I extended a hand. She looked away from me, determined to take care of herself.

"Right," I whispered. "Come with me, and put that mask back on."

She hesitated for a moment before she decided she would follow me. I took stock of the caves in front of us. I wondered if they were inhabited. Picking up two rocks from the ground, I leaned in front of the entrance and knocked the stones together. Would anything react?

The sounds of shuffling feet and angry growls came out of the cave. We quickly retreated. I wiped off the sweat trickling down the side of my face with the back of my arm.

"Are you all right back there?"

I peeked at Gabriella from the mirror on my weapon. She made a dismissive noise with her tongue. The rag over my mouth flapped when I let out a frustrated sigh. I shifted my neck to my right and flicked my head toward a northbound trail.

"Let's go this way."

I could hear her wheezing breath behind me as I took the lead. Before night settled across the leaden skies and washed out the faint light, I found an empty cave. It wasn't large, but looked spacious enough and was nicely located behind a small stream and waterfall. We wouldn't be thirsty, at least. I brushed aside the withered vines and fallen branches obstructing the entrance. Several minutes had passed, but Gabriella had still not said another word.

I got down on one knee and moved my satchel in front of me. Rifling through my tools, I pulled an emergency light from the bottom of the bag. I twisted the red cap on the end of the cylinder, revealing a white button. When I touched it twice, a bright light shot out from the end. I held it over my head like a torch and entered the cave.

"You can rest there," I said gruffly, pointing to a dry spot in the back of the cave. Setting the light against the wall, I added, "The emergency light should last until I return. I won't be long."

I unloaded some ammunition to lighten my satchel before heading back out the cave. Tapping a bronze star pinned to my chest pocket activated a flashlight. It would illuminate my path and reveal boulders and deep fissures in the cracked earth.

I went around the obstacles and made my way to the water source behind the cave. The water looked clear and delicious. I reached out my hands to scoop a drink, and it tasted better than I could have imagined. Satisfied, I took out two empty containers and filled them from the stream. I returned to the cave with the water, setting my satchel on the opposite corner from Gabriella.

Her side of the cave looked empty. I had one jug of water with me as a peace offering. But as I knelt down next to her to hand over the water, she flinched away from me. Her shoulders moved back, and I noticed a momentary look of fear in her eyes once again. Not knowing what to do, I set the jug down beside her and nodded brusquely before retreating.

I lay on the floor and propped my back against the wall. My emergency travel supplies poked out from the side of my satchel. I ripped off the seal and proceeded to inflate a stuffed pillow and unroll a thin blanket. I piled the items behind her before creeping meekly out of the cave again.

This was not how I wanted to start things between us.

CHAPTER 6

GABRIELLA

Have you ever tried sleeping on a cave floor? It was more comfortable that I had expected, but I barely slept a wink all night. The ultra-thin blanket Laz left me felt about as thick as a sheet of toilet paper, but it was warm. I felt like I had a wool garment wrapped around me.

I found myself trapped in a shitty catch-22 of being exhausted as all hell but unable to get the sleep I desperately needed. Instead, I stared into the dark of my closed eyelids. Frantic memories raced through my mind, and I couldn't stop thinking.

The last time I had these problems was when Ronnie was my neighbor. He was an untalented dirtbag who lived in the upstairs apartment when I used to live with Jake. Getting well-rested before I had to get up for work was impossible when the sounds of a struggling artist playing grating 'music' into the dead of the night filled the apartment.

I opened my eyes reluctantly. They adjusted to the bright yellow glow of the emergency light stuck against the wall. The only companion around was my shadow. I sighed. Laz was still out.

I knitted my eyebrows together and peered out at the faint traces of light streaking across the hazy sky. It was almost daybreak. Great. My first sunrise on a wretched alien planet. How romantic. The thought of starting a new day made me shudder.

59

My head fell back on a small pillow. What could be keeping him away for so long? I fluffed the pillow absent-mindedly.

Although I was grateful for the rescue, I wasn't sure how I felt about Laz. I couldn't get a read on him for the life of me. I felt shaken up when he exploded.

To be fair, I supposed I could have kept my mouth shut and given him time to process what was going on around him. I wondered if I had caught him at the wrong time or if he had an unstable, explosive temper. What if my encounter was merely a taste of what was coming in the future?

I was responsible for everything that was happening to me. What was I thinking? How could I have accepted someone's hand in marriage without knowing anything about him? He was my husband already and the facts I knew about him could be counted on one hand. For all I knew, I had married a psychopathic serial killer, and I was going to be another one of his wives who met an untimely demise.

Even though it was a stereotypical premise, it could be true. That would explain why he chose me so quickly in the first place. Had he given the marriage any thought at all? Why else would he have chosen me out of all the other TerraMates brides?

Maybe trusting my gut was reckless and stupid. I rubbed my head, thinking about all the information I knew about Laz. The Maztek army men answered to him, so he was a commander. Early on, I thought he was a man of few words. Now that I had interacted with him, it seemed he was a man of no words. It had even crossed my mind that he might not speak much Standard, but now I knew that was not the case.

'Sorry' didn't seem to be part of his vocabulary, although he did leave me with light, water, and bedding before he abandoned me for the night. I would have appreciated it more if he had told me what time he would be back, but I enjoyed the comforts.

Other than that, I had a blank for the rest of Laz's profile. What were his likes and dislikes? What was his family like? Did he have brothers? Sisters? A drunk great-uncle? Did he drink his coffee black, or with sugar? Did caffeine even exist on Maztek? The unanswered questions in mind were coming far too late to help.

I clucked testily and lifted my back off the ground. Unscrewing the jug, I took a large gulp of refreshingly cold water. My eyes flicked to the empty cave entrance and back to the ground.

I draped the blanket around me like a cape and huddled up against the wall. Damn it. Where was he?

Laz had returned briefly during the night for a couple of minutes before disappearing again. Groggy but lucid, I had peeked out from under my covers to observe him in action. After he had crept back into the cave, he made a beeline for a knapsack of weapons. I was surprised by how much he could fit into a seemingly bottomless bag and wanted one for myself. I didn't feel comfortable asking him for one or borrowing something.

It felt creepy pretending to be asleep while I observed him, but I didn't want him to know I was awake.

I realized something was off when I heard him suppressing grunts of pain. I had noticed earlier that he was favoring one of his arms. There were jagged teeth marks along his right bicep, and electric-blue alien blood jetted out of the puncture wound.

I watched as Laz poked around in his bag until he found a square silver case. He split the case open with one hand and removed a thick syringe filled with green liquid. Gross. I've always been squeamish about shots and this one looked painful. I didn't know what was in the needle, but after he stuck it into his arm and injected the green liquid, his wound started healing itself. Within a few seconds, his arm looked as good as new. I had to look carefully to see a faint scar on his bicep.

Mazteks were fascinating creatures. During the explosion and the ensuing chaos with the Xylo guards, I noticed that the Maztek had come out virtually unscathed. My heart had jumped every time I saw one of the Maztek fall over or land on their backs, but they would spring right off the floor every time.

One Maztek warrior had fallen over the edge of a multiple-story drop but was fighting at the side of his crew minutes later. I watched him slash the throats of two Xylo guards soon after. Their bodies were tough and resilient, but I assumed that a deep cut could be fatal, even for them.

It looked like Laz had lost a lot of blood from the bite, and it had needed immediate treatment. I realized some of his blue blood stained the walls of the cave.

There was one thing I couldn't ignore, and it was something I didn't want to admit to myself. He looked drastically sexier in person, and I wasn't prepared for the reality of his presence. I couldn't explain it in words, but the night before I couldn't help but break out in a cold sweat as I watched him heal his body. As soon as the fear subsided, I was unable to look away from him.

His face was shiny with sweat and his jaw clenched while he patched up the wound. I knew he hurt but wasn't giving into the pain. His silent but heavily breathing body oozed masculinity, and part of me responded to it.

I have never been the type to get all hot and bothered by manly, peacocking men who paraded their bravado on their sleeves, but Laz was different. The way he calmly took control of the situation and managed it without making excuses or complaints made my toes curl.

When Jake came home one night after a liquor-binging escapade, he had stubbed his toe on the end of our coffee table. From the crash in the living room and subsequent whining, you would have thought his leg had been cut off. I was asleep in our bedroom at the time, but I instantly woke up. For the briefest of moments, I thought a toddler had wandered into our apartment and taken control of Jake's body.

When I rushed out to the living room after hastily throwing my bathrobe on inside-out, I found a red-faced

Jake on the floor cradling his big toe. Full-fledged tears were flowing down his face, and he reeked of vodka and vomit. The pathetic image of an unemployed, full-grown man crying out for his mommy made me cringe.

Snap.

My ears perked up. I hopefully glanced over at the cave entrance. The whistling breeze rustled a few branches across the floor.

"Hello? Is someone anyone there?"

A figure cast an enormous shadow over the entrance, its shoulders and legs spaced apart in a threatening stance. I choked on my words and fled to a corner of the cave. It was Laz, but he looked deadly.

Loose, dark waves of hair were matted and stuck to his face. The rag which once protected his lungs hung loosely around his neck. Splatters of bright red blood covered his face and uniform. The scent in the air started to change, becoming thick with the sour, metallic stench of fresh blood. My eyes zeroed in on a knife in his left hand. The blade dripped a scarlet red liquid, the same color I saw on his body and clothes.

I let out a small scream. "Are you okay? Why is there so much blood?"

Laz dropped the knife to the ground and reached outside the cave. Using both hands, he hoisted a large, furry carcass into the room, leaving it only a few feet from the entrance. I swallowed my screams and fought to regain control of myself.

The kill was a plump two-headed animal with two sets of antlers and spotted yellow fur. There was hardly any blood on its hide. In fact, there were no signs of an entry wound other than the gutting of the animal, but it appeared to have been cut after death. There was a clean break in the animal's neck. The creature's glossy green eyes looked peaceful and unaware of their demise.

"Sorry." I tried to look calm. I tugged on the ends of my hair skittishly. "You startled me."

"It's fine," Laz replied.

He grabbed his bag and pulled out a small gray cloth the size of a face towel. As he rubbed it against his face, the towel began to absorb all the animal blood on him. He walked back to the entrance and wrung out the rag outside the cave.

"What took you so long? You were gone the whole night."

"It took time for me to find this poor fellow. He was the only healthy one in the herd. All the other winoas I saw were half-dead or diseased, so their meat would have been inedible. I did find a couple of wild triple-horned boars, but I had to keep my distance. Those things looked rabid and seemed intent on eating each other."

"You know what? Forget I asked," I mumbled, suppressing a gag.

I couldn't be sure, but I thought I saw a hint of a smile cross his lips. After he had gotten himself cleaned up, he left the cave and returned carrying wood bark, shavings, and twigs for a fire. I folded the blanket sloppily on my lap and set it aside. By the time I joined him, he already had a flame going in the center of the cave. He fed the fire with more twigs and sticks until he had a controlled burn going.

I sat across him with crossed legs. Unsure of how to strike up a proper, civil conversation with this stranger, and not sure what to talk about even if I did, I kept my mouth shut. I turned my attention the fire and snapped a few more twigs to toss into the flames.

Laz poured water from a jug onto his knife to wash it out. It didn't seem much cleaner to me. He cut some bloody chunks of the pink winoa meat and stuck two sharpened twigs through it. I mumbled a quick "thank you" as he handed it to me before fixing one for himself.

A bizarre thought crept into my mind. This was what the witch from Hansel and Gretel had done. She had showered the kids with truckloads of candy to fatten them up for a wonderful feast for herself. I pushed the crazy thought out of my head and held my twigs over the fire with both hands. Out of the corner of my eye, I looked at Laz suspiciously. I hoped he wasn't going to eat me.

"You're going to want to roast it on all sides slowly and thoroughly like a rotisserie. Winoas are usually excellent when cooked medium rare, but I wouldn't recommend doing that on this planet. If it turns golden-brown, you'll know it's cooked enough to eat."

"Thanks for the tip."

"The meat will be slightly bland, but we'll have to make do."

"That's fine. We're lucky to have anything to eat. I'm sure it will be delicious. I mean, I've had leftover chicken my ex...roommate made before and that tasted like feet."

"I wasn't aware that humans ate feet," he said absentmindedly. He removed a metal disk from his bag and manipulated the ends, forming a pot without a handle. He proceeded to pour the remaining water from his jug into the pot. As the water started to heat up, he sliced off some meat with his knife and added it to the water. I stared at him.

"No, I meant — never mind. Just for the record, we don't eat feet."

"Whatever you say, Earth girl."

We finished roasting our winoa meat and ate our meals in silence. As the aromatic scent of cooked meat wafted into my nostrils, I suddenly felt light-headed. My stomach decided it was the appropriate time to announce how hungry I was. I carefully massaged my belly, but it was intent on rumbling no matter what I did.

My eyes shifted toward Laz, who was too busy eating his meal to notice anything about me. I sipped on the bowl of bone stock he handed me, wetting my lips. The meat was surprisingly tender and juicy. Maybe it was my hunger talking, but everything tasted delicious.

Laz burped, pounding on his chest as he rose to his feet. He was so tall that he had to hold his head at an angle to keep it from hitting the ceiling. Flicking off the black liquid that had plopped on his nose from overhead, he moved to the corner of the cave. He shrugged off the top of his stained uniform and his black tank top, tossing them aside.

I swallowed at the sight of his body, looking at the sinewy ripples of his flexed back. Crossing one leg over the other, I quickly shifted my focus to the clear soup in my hands. As I slurped down the soup, I couldn't stop my eyes from drifting back to Laz. The steam from my soup was increasing the heat in my face.

His body was so sculpted that it seemed like he was a creation brought to life. A giant tattoo of a wheel spanned his entire back, intricately detailed with ancient Maztekki symbols and scripts. It danced along when his muscles moved.

I watched Laz gather hair out of his face and tie it up again in his usual bun. Sliding a couple of knives into his belt, he grabbed onto one of the animal's antlers and dragged it toward the entrance. He looked back at me, smoothing his beard with his free hand.

"There's a stream and small waterfall behind the cave. You can take the jug if you get thirsty again. The container will automatically sterilize the water. If you want to wash in the stream, there's a bar of soap somewhere in my bag. Take the mask with you and don't take it off for long. I'll be back soon."

I nodded, waving half-heartedly to his back as he trotted off. After treating myself to two more pieces of meat and finishing the soup before the fire died out, I took Laz up on his offer. My body felt disgusting. I dug out an unscented bar of soap and headed out to find the waterfall.

The waterfall and stream behind the cave weren't as good as the lake by Grandma Molly's house, but they were something. I stretched my arms behind me, attempting to scratch an obnoxious itch hovering in an impossible-to-reach spot. Failing, I groaned. I looked around to see if anyone was watching me. There was absolutely no one around me. I took off the mask, stripped off my clothes, and placed them on a boulder next to the falling water.

I grabbed the soap and braced myself before stepping into the water. It was freezing! I stood shivering in the water until my body adjusted to the temperature. Taking the bar of soap, I whipped my wet hair out of my face and started to scrub myself down. The water instantly relieved the itch on my back.

I thought I might never feel clean again, but I was getting there. I rubbed the soap on my head and started lathering it into my hair.

As I set down the bar of soap, I thought I heard the crackle of a twig. My eyes flew open. I gazed around me, but there was nobody there. Sighing, I cursed under my breath and went back to washing my hair. My fatigue was starting to play tricks on me.

Or was there someone else out here with us?

CHAPTER 7

LAZ

One of the heels on Gabriella's shoes had broken off while she was running. I was no shoemaker, but the only other person around wasn't one either. I thought I would be able to rig up something with an animal pelt to piece together a pair of slippers for her. They weren't anything you would see in a fashion show, but I was able to put laces into the opening, so she could adjust them, at least.

Apart from the shoes, I brought along some whittling tools to create any additional hand weapons I would need. I turned the winoa bones into sharp triangles which could function as arrowheads or knives. We would get more than food from the kill.

When I was finished creating weapons of destruction, my hands stunk to the heavens. I laid my tools out on the ground and set out to find a stream and rinse the smell off my fingers. The walk back up the trail felt longer than the climb down.

I knew the wildlife was the same in either direction, but it felt like I was fending off a different species of insect each step of the way. Earlier, I had to catch myself from falling backward when a four-headed magfly the size of my thumb buzzed past my face. The insects were big, but they were slow and lazy. This planet had so many problems even its insects were deformed and diseased. Every moment I was here helped me understand why my Maztek ancestors had decided to leave Xylox and form a new civilization on a different planet.

71

I reached the top of the trail. As I stuck out my hands to balance myself, I stopped. A mask and a small mountain of women's clothes covered the stone I was about to grab. I squinted at the waterfall and stopped moving when I saw what was under it.

Gabriella stood, water rushing over her body, and she was completely naked. She faced away from me. I imagined her eyes were closed. I watched her fingers weave through her hair as she washed away the bubbles. My eyes dropped down to the smooth curves of her round, squeezable ass. The sight took my cock by surprise, too. It swelled and began poking its tip against my thigh.

A guilty flush covered my cheeks. I moved away from the rock and started walking away from Gabriella. I knew I shouldn't look, but my saluting member wanted me to go into the water with her.

I searched my mind for all the tactics I once used to ward off erections from when I was an adolescent. First, I computed random mathematical equations in my head. That shield turned out to be useless when the side-view image of Gabriella's hot body snuck back into my thoughts. I had caught sight of her puffy, pink nipples for a second. Her breasts weren't gigantic, but they were beautifully shaped. I reached into the waistband of my pants to adjust my throbbing cock.

Cracking my neck, I tried to distract myself again. I attempted to recall the names of the forty-two states on Maztek. Fallgold, Marblemere, Starryedge, Hollowbrook, Zumleigh... I wasn't sure what it was about the thumb-sized heart tattooed on Gabriella's right hip, but it was absurdly sexy. She had a great pair of legs, too. Those muscular thighs and shapely calves looked even better soaking wet. I stopped moving and started to imagine what her legs would look like wrapped around my neck.

I rubbed at my temples, grunting. What was the matter with me? I was a grown male – these lustful thoughts should have been in my past. The last time I felt this uncomfortably aroused was over twenty years ago.

She was technically my wife, and we had both signed off on a TerraMates marriage certificate that finalized our wedding. Even so, there was something inexplicably unethical about watching Gabriella when she was most vulnerable. I suppose my father and his father, my Upa, contributed to my guilt. From an early age, they explained to me in exquisite detail what they would do to me if I were to disrespect a woman.

But more importantly, I was nothing but a stranger to her.

I knew there was a chance that she might have been cleaning, but I assumed she would be washing her feet or arms. The last thing I imagined was her being nude out in the middle of the woods. Why would she think it was a good idea to be naked in enemy territory? My eyes rolled up to the heavens. I had been in the company of Gabriella for less than two days, but her erratic and unpredictable decisions were already starting to drive me up the wall.

The thought triggered the memory of Marshall Hathaway. He was the only other human I had ever known. Up until this point, I presumed the majority of Earthlings were level-headed and pragmatic by nature, as he was. Apart from Upa and my father, Marshall was the only other man who ever gave a damn about me.

As for my mother, I never knew the lady and didn't care to learn more about her. She had disappeared soon after I was born and never returned. I was raised by Upa and my father until they were both killed in the Fallgold incident twenty-five years ago.

Marshall was part of a small community of humans stationed on Maztek. The man was intelligent and sincere, which garnered the respect of Upa and my father. The three had met a couple of years before I was born. The way I heard it, they became instant friends.

Even though Marshall was not a fighter, he always accompanied them when they went out on the field. He risked his life numerous times in different Xylo war zones tending to injured warriors. When the frequency of the Xylo attacks decreased, he dedicated his time to helping Maztek in impoverished villages afflicted with mysterious and debilitating diseases.

When my blood family perished in the Fallgold battle, Marshall made sure to check on me when he could. He never tried to refill the hole Upa and my father left in my life, but he acknowledged it existed. That was all I needed. The visits were brief, but they remained some of the most pleasant memories I had.

In a cruel twist of fate, Marshall died a horrible death under the hand of Synic. Synic had taken command in place of his father, Dyron, who perished in Fallgold. Thirsting for blood and having something to prove, Synic executed

Marshall when he refused to give up information he knew about the Maztek forces.

The deaths of all three males in my life had a long-lasting effect on me. I knew I needed to be the one to take down those Xylo sons of bitches. I joined a military academy funded by Maztek royalty and began training at the age of fifteen.

I made a left turn, heading back to camp. Now that I was thinking about Marshall, I remembered one time I had seen his composure challenged. The man had a reputation for a consistently chipper mood and the ability to keep calm under pressure, making him respected by most Maztek. His exterior remained stoic and calm through Upa and my father's death, but it was finally put to the test two months after Fallgold.

Treating thousands of dying Maztek civilians had preoccupied him, making him miss the birth of his daughter. At the time, he hadn't seen me, but I was lurking in the back of the stock room when he burst inside on one of his breaks. Not knowing what to do, I hid behind one of the massive containers.

Without warning, I saw the person I knew as an unbreakable, happy-go-lucky man collapse on the ground. He sobbed more than I had ever seen any grown man cry. The sound of helpless emotion in his voice was unforgettable.

I suppose even he had a breaking point.

Maybe I needed to rethink my strategy with Gabriella. At this stage, I hoped an open-minded approach would work. It would be in both of our best interests if I put in the effort to make her journey to a foreign, war-torn planet a little more pleasant.

It was an uncomfortable feeling. I had been looking for my naima for many years. Now that I had the chance for companionship, I realized I was unprepared. It was like being a rookie all over again. I could only rely on what I knew – to improvise, conquer, and overcome whatever situation came my way.

I wasn't sure what to do, but I knew I didn't want to scare her away forever.

As I inched closer to the cave, something made me halt in my tracks. I moved into a crouch and concealed myself behind the trunk of a tree. The pungent odor of rotting fruit drifted down from above, penetrating the rag on my face and burning in my nose. I fixed the rag's knot behind my head and put my hands on the tree trunk as I looked at our camp from a distance.

A pair of Xylo hitchhikers hobbled out of the cave on their hands and feet. One carried winoa meat in his pockets and under his arms. The other had his hands full with a pot of bone stock.

One Xylo had a green eye and a brown one. He barked to his companion in a high-pitched local dialect. The other screeched in agreement. The pair moved east toward an inclined path.

They were headed straight for the waterfall and Gabriella.

CHAPTER 8

GABRIELLA

"Crap!" I caught the square of soap just before it slipped through my fingers. My lips broke out into a grin at my small victory, but I embraced it. It was the first genuine smile that had crossed my face since my arrival on this godforsaken planet. I rubbed the wrinkled tips of my fingers with my other hand. My quick shower had taken much longer than had intended.

I set the soap down on a rock and moved into the path of falling water to rinse off one final time. A soft pop sounded from my back as I bent forward to wash the lather off my legs.

What occurred next happened so fast, it caught me completely off-guard.

The noise of sudden, rushed movement filled my ears. My fingertips were moved from my calves in one swift motion. A pair of sweaty, hulking arms closed in over me and tackled me to the ground.

To a bystander, it all happened within a few seconds, but it felt like the moment lasted forever. I flopped around like a struggling fish out of water, trying to get a look at my attacker.

"Laz? I was just relaxing! And I'm naked!"

He rolled me on top of him and hooked his feet over my ankles to prevent any movement. He used his arms to prevent my limbs from flailing.

"Be quiet," he whispered. "We're not alone."

He had his hand over my mouth, so it wasn't like I could say anything. His fingers stunk. No matter how much he washed, he wouldn't be able to clean himself from the stench of the winoa kill. Was he trying to have his way with me?

"Damn it, Gabriella. Stop struggling. And try not to make any noise!"

"Mmmphhh!" Every instinct I had told me to move away and hide. I didn't know what to do, but I didn't want to be here. Maybe I hadn't recovered from the crash landing. My mind was aflutter, and I couldn't think straight.

All I knew was that I needed to get myself out of this situation. I wanted to survive. I was not going to let myself be captured again.

I bared my teeth frantically and positioned them over the flesh between his thumb and his index finger. I had my mouth open, ready to bite down and run when two figures crept into the side of my view. I turned to look at the new sight.

It was two Xylo. I guess we weren't alone after all.

One was female. Her thinning and unwashed hair hung in loose clumps over the back of her enlarged head. The male Xylo's left eye nearly made my meal of winoa meat come back up my throat. His eye had yellow gunk and was half-eaten by chubby maggots that appeared to have set up a permanent residence in his skull. They looked malnourished, and their oversized clothing made them look bony as well. Dirt covered the backs of their necks and their faces were marked with multiple scabs.

I felt muscles start to relax slowly. Laz had loosened his grip over my mouth the moment I finally stopped resisting. What was more, this whole time, he didn't have an erection. I guess he wasn't trying to rape me after all.

All the pieces quickly fell into place. The thumping of my irregular heartbeat began to slow down to its normal pace.

I turned my attention back to the Xylo intruders. My eyes fell on the familiar pot and sacks of raw pink meat they carried. Behind Laz's hand, my jaw opened. I watched bitterly as the Xylos discarded the delicious soup onto the ground and filled the pot with water. They tipped the rims of the pot toward their faces and caught the water messily with wagging purple tongues. Freeloading seemed to be universal. Why hadn't Laz done anything to stop or scare off these good-for-nothing scavengers?

A tingling sensation arising from my gut disrupted my thoughts. With my nerves finally settling, I abruptly realized I was completely naked. Laz's sweaty chest was pressed up against me. I could feel his heart beating against my back.

Now that I wasn't actively moving away from him, he had switched his hold around my arms. He held my wrists together with his closed fists, but his arms were raised slightly above my heaving breasts. He didn't have a hard-on, but I could still feel the length of his cock through his pants. As he shifted underneath me, my thighs clenched involuntarily. I could feel the solid ridges of his washboard stomach muscles gently brushing against the flesh of my lower back.

I felt the walls of my pussy contracting. Now I was losing control of my body. A dribble of my pussy juices oozed out against my will, lubricating my sex. I couldn't explain the conflicted feelings of arousal pulsing through my body.

The sensation triggered a buzz in my left ear once again, and I could feel my cheeks heating up as they turned pink. Part of me liked how everything felt, but a smarter part of me knew this was neither the place nor time for intimacy.

As luck would have it, an insufferable itch appeared on my ankle.

In my position, all I could do was nudge one ankle against the other and try to rub them together. But as I adjusted my hips, his cock fell into my butt crack. My hips ground against him as I maneuvered to scratch myself. I started to feel his stiffening length swell in the cushion of my cheeks.

"The coast is clear. You can get off me now."

I wonder if you were getting off already, I thought to myself. I rolled off of Laz right away. Glancing to my right between two mossy boulders, I saw the little backs of the retreating aliens. Laz reached for my clothes, turning away as he handed them to me. I grabbed my clothes and dressed with lightning speed before he turned around.

"Are you going to let them get away with our stuff?" I asked him curiously. My forehead wrinkled.

"Affirmative," grunted Laz. He took the bar of soap and started to scrub off the smell from his fingers under the waterfall.

"But why?"

"They're not our enemy," Laz replied without skipping a beat. His eyes remained focused on his hands, but I thought I could hear a hint of emotion in his tone. "They were just hungry."

The raw honesty in his words made me ashamed I had asked about their future.

"That's a good point. I guess I'm paranoid from my only other Xylo encounter."

"Next time you want to prance around naked in the middle of enemy territory, I suggest you let me know ahead of time. It will be easier for me to take care of you if I know you're going to do something stupid before anything happens."

"Excuse me? I can look after myself, thank you very much. Wait, where are you going?"

"Back to the cave. Where else?"

"There you go. Walking away from me again in the middle of a conversation. No surprise there." I sighed at the sight of Laz's back growing smaller in the distance.

* * * *

"Thirty-eight...thirty-nine...forty."

The moment my body touched the ground, I felt a wave of relief wash over me. I didn't even move my arms. They were still crossed against my chest as I slowly caught my breath. My calf muscles were starting to get tired. They had been propped up against the wall for over thirty minutes. I placed my fingers into the slight hollows of my abs and examined the work-in-progress.

Satisfied, I swung my legs off the wall and sat up. I reached for my water jug to replenish the sweat I had lost from my workout. With Laz doing his own thing for most of the day, I was left to find ways to entertain myself.

I set the jug down next to me. This boredom was enough to drive anyone to tears. What was I supposed to do around here all day?

I poked around in the open box of supplies Laz left laying around and found a couple of thick, multipurpose bands. Holding the bands between my hands, I pulled them apart to test their durability. I leaned back against the wall and gathered the front part of my hair. As I settled into the silence, I began to braid my hair lazily.

"What the fuck do you think you're doing?"

I jumped off the ground immediately. My hands fell to my sides. Laz was standing by the cave entrance. The daylight struck him at an angle that made his upper body appear cloaked in shadows.

"I was just fixing my hair."

My teeth were chattering, and I was stuttering uncontrollably. Laz moved toward me and stopped next to his open toolbox. He whipped around and scowled at me expectantly, waiting for an explanation.

Why was he so angry? He was acting like I had disrespected his mother. I knew I shouldn't have been poking around in his tool box in the first place, but this was too much. I was starting to get ticked off by his cocky attitude. I hadn't signed up to live in a cave.

I rolled my eyes and turned away from him. "I'm sorry," I started, beginning to reconstruct my braid.

"No, you're not," snarled Laz from behind me. "But you will be."

"What is that supposed to mean?"

Laz descended on me from behind, putting a hand over my nose and mouth. I clawed at his arms with weak fingers that slipped off him. That wasn't going to work. I stomped on the toes of his boots with the heels of my bare feet with all my might, but all that did was hurt my foot. I tried to demand that he move. My howling disappeared in the suffocating curve of his arm.

I shoved the back of my head against his chest and dug my nails into his arm. Feeling his grip loosen, I slid my head out the gap of his elbow.

"Get off me, Laz! What do you think you're doing? This isn't funny."

"Do you think I find it amusing that you came in here and disrespected me and my property?"

"I'm not disrespecting anybody! Are you crazy? I'm sorry! Please. Let me go. I'll do anything."

Laz released me from his hold. I slid to the ground, landing on my hands and feet. My braids had unraveled in the commotion. I had struggled with him so much that I could see little jewels of blood in my fingertips.

"What are you going to do for me?" asked Laz matter-of-factly. He roughly stroked the bristles of his beard.

"I don't know. I'm already down here. Do you want me to drop and give you twenty push-ups?"

Laz's low, dry chuckle sent an icy blast through the pit of my gut. "Almost funny, but not quite, Earthling."

"What do you want?"

I gulped back the rest of my words. Laz's smoldering green eyes were looking at my face, but they lingered on my mouth. I gaped at him, staring at the bulge visible through his pants. His gaze was fixated on my mouth as he unfastened his pants and kicked them aside.

A tight black loincloth barely covered his full-blown erection.

My panties were moist. Shame and embarrassment smacked me in the face, but I couldn't help it. The thickness of his cock prominently protruded through the stretchy material of his loincloth. I peeled my eyes away from the swollen package between his legs and pushed all the shamefully dirty thoughts to the back of my mind.

What was wrong with me? I shouldn't like this or get turned on by it.

"Take off your clothes."

"What? But I..."

"Did I fucking stutter?" Laz spat at me. He bent down on one knee and looked into my face. I knew he was strikingly handsome, but from this angle and distance, I realized he was frightening as well. "That was an order."

He didn't shout, but for some reason, his lowered voice was more terrifying. I got to my feet, and I realized I was shaking like I never had before. I unzipped the back of my stained pastel dress. My shoulders emerged one at a time. A blast of cold open air embraced me as my dress fell around my navel.

I had to wiggle to pull it down over my hips. Instinctively, I moved my hands to cover my exposed boobs and my wet pussy lips. I nervously twiddled with the smooth ends of my light blonde pubes, feeling vulnerable and nude in the middle of a strange cave.

"At ease."

I lifted my arms slowly and tucked them behind my back.

"Feet apart. Straighten your back," Laz commanded scathingly. "I should let you have it right now for that shit stance you're giving me."

I obeyed immediately and placed my feet shoulder-length apart. Laz circled me repeatedly holding his arms behind his back. He made soft grunts of approval as he inspected me from head to toe. I could feel his burning eyes looking over every inch of my body. It was taking every ounce of self-control I had not to move a muscle or make the smallest sound.

Laz slapped a hand on my left breast and gave it an abrasive, hearty squeeze. I bit down on my tongue and curled my toes as his fingers clamped down on my puffy nipples. He leaned in close to me, watching my reaction as he jerked them back and twisted them. His lips opened as he watched me struggle to contain all my sounds and reactions. My glazed eyes looked straight ahead. Something told me he was genuinely enjoying my discomfort.

He smacked an open hand against my left butt cheek. He gripped it so hard I imagined his fingertips disappearing into my flesh. I gasped at the sting, but made the mistake of lifting my eyes off the ground and taking a peek at him.

"What the hell do you think you're looking at? Get down on your knees."

I slunk back down to the ground. A coat of dirt from the cave floors covered my kneecaps. I found my mouth stretching open without prompting - I didn't want to get yelled at again. Laz laughed darkly as he began to remove his loincloth.

"Good, good. It looks like someone's finally learning."

My open lips began to tremble at the girth of his cock, but I didn't have time think about what I was doing. Before I knew it, I felt a hand grab my head by the hair. I felt him pulling me forward.

His thick, veined muscle forced its way between my lips. I gagged and swirled my tongue around the pole pumping in and out of my mouth. His balls knocked against my chin as he rammed his cock into the constricting passage of my throat. I reached up to slow him down, wrapping my fist around the base of his erection.

I didn't realize cock could taste this good.

Moans floated out of me, sounding like a stranger's to my ears. Laz lifted one of his feet and pried open my legs so he could get a better view of me. He traced his toe against the stream trickling down my thighs.

"You're enjoying this, aren't you? Why don't you come over here so I can take care of you."

"Wait! Stop."

I pulled away from him and started crawling off in the opposite direction. Laz grabbed me by the ankles and yanked me toward him. He overpowered me, sliding my thighs open and positioning my ass cheeks in midair.

"Laz!"

* * * *

My body jolted awake. I scanned my surroundings with an intense, wide-eyed gaze. My heartbeat was racing through my body, and it only started to slow down when I began to make sense of everything around me.

The cave walls glowed faintly from the emergency light stick. The only sound was the soft crackling of the dying fire next to me. I exhaled slowly and tossed the thin blanket off me as I sat up against the wall.

I had been dreaming, but somehow I felt disappointed. I didn't want Laz to take me like that. Did I?

As I tried to analyze my Freudian dream, my tired eyes fell to a pair of yellow objects on the ground to my right. I felt a pulse through my body as I scooped up the crudely made winoa pelt slippers from the ground. The insides were even lined with a soft insole for my sore feet. I wondered where Laz had found the new shoes.

I looked at Laz's sleeping figure on the opposite side of the fizzling fire. He had one arm casually swung over his eyes. His mouth was slightly ajar in deep slumber. I fingered the furry yellow pelt of my slippers. What a thoughtful gift.

Even though I was still exhausted, I couldn't go back to sleep.

CHAPTER 9

LAZ

"Let's go! We haven't got all day!"

I needed to find a way to repair my communicator, and we were running out of daylight on Xylox. Either Gabriella was taking her sweet time or humans were naturally slower than Maztek. Either way, we were taking too long.

"I'm doing the best I can over here," Gabriella grumbled sourly from behind me. "Maybe you could remember that my legs are half your size."

"That's no excuse. Wyla's only four feet ten inches, and she outruns all my men. I thought Earth women liberated themselves and were men's equals."

"Oh yeah? Well, good for her," Gabriella shot back, putting a hand on her chest. She paused. "I stand by what I said. If I'm slowing you down so much, why don't you sweep me off my feet again and carry me there? While you're at it, why don't you wipe my ass?"

I squatted into position in front of her and flexed my back muscles.

"What are you doing?" asked Gabriella. I could feel her penetrating gaze boring into my back.

"You need a ride? Get on."

"No way. You can get up now. I was being facetious, damn it. I know how to walk. You lead the way and only start worrying if I'm not within a hundred feet of you."

"Suit yourself." With a shrug, I got up off the ground and swung my satchel over my back. I had spent a few hours staking out the terrain yesterday, and my efforts were paying off now. The trail leading to the underbelly of the Xylo city was due west from our cave's water source. Gabriella and I had figured out the shortest route to the city that would minimize the chances of any Xylo contact.

We had been on the road for a while now, but I thought we were close to the checkpoint. It was only another couple of miles. I narrowed my eyes when I saw a blue ribbon tied around a tree trunk on my right. The sight of my trail marker energized me, and I moved toward the stump quickly, making a flurry of dead leaves. When I reached the tree, I untied the knot and slipped the ribbon into my pocket, adding it to the other scraps of fabric.

"Make sure I notice you if you start to lose me."

"Of course. I wouldn't want you abandoning me in an alien wasteland."

I moved on, eagerly searching for the next ribbon. Soon I heard a squawk of pain behind me. I turned around on my heel just in time to see Gabriella's feet start sinking into the earth. She tripped and tumbled forward but caught herself before she crashed into the ground. Her gas mask fell over her head and rolled to a stop next to her.

"Shit!"

I jogged back to Gabriella at once to help her ease her foot out from the hole. Her handmade shoes weren't the best for hiking, of course. Her feet were cushioned but the fall made her ankle turn pink. It was swelling already. I checked her face.

Gabriella looked nervous. I wrapped my fingers around her ankle and gingerly felt around it.

"Hold still and try to relax," I crooned. "This is going to hurt, but I'll make it as quick as possible."

"It's okay. I can do it myself."

Gabriella pulled my fingers off her leg. Before I could stop her, she carefully grabbed onto her swollen ankle. She squeezed her eyes shut, grunting as she twisted her ankle sharply to her right. A loud pop sounded in the air as her sprained fibula twisted back into place. A single tear leaked out from the corner of her eye and clung to her lashes, but I didn't hear a noise. Her eyelids fluttered like she was blinking away the pain.

I reached into my satchel and took out a flat square packet. A rectangular chunk solidified in the sealed package when I twisted off the nozzle. I tore off the top and allowed bursts of cold smoke to steam out from the opening.

"That's amazing!"

"It's just a cold compress." I took the ice and pressed it against her ankle. "Hold this here to stop the swelling."

"Thanks," said Gabriella. She let out a moan of contentment as she stretched her leg. "That feels so much better than before."

"The pain should subside in less than an hour," I told her as I wrapped her ankle. "Do you think you can still walk?"

"We'll just have to see, won't we?" Gabriella chirped with fake optimism. She hoisted herself up to her feet and started to fall. "Nope, going down...whoa!"

I moved behind her and caught her by the shoulders. "You're in no shape to go anywhere right now," I said, shaking my head. I tried to keep a lecturing tone of accusation out of my voice. "I suppose taking some time off to rest wouldn't hurt. I've got another light to last us the rest of the way, but we'll have to stay close together."

"Sounds like a plan. I'm starving."

I eased the gas mask back on Gabriella's head. Slinging her arm over my shoulder, I lifted her off the ground and moved away from the path to the city. I loaded my belongings on top of her and carried everything to the far side of the hill. I unloaded my equipment. She cried out as I dumped her onto my pile of stuff.

"Ow! Thanks for the heads up," said Gabriella sarcastically. She patted the ground before sitting back.

I reached my hand into the satchel and pulled out some rations.

"Karbachi or mandala?"

"Excuse me?"

"Spicy or sweet?"

"Sweet, I guess. I don't care. I'm so hungry that I think I'd eat anything right now."

I unwrapped the mandala bar and passed it to her.

She took a careful bite. "Not too shabby." The wrapper crinkled noisily in her hand as she hungrily chewed the flaky bar. "I don't know what the purple shell on the outside is, but the filling tastes like fudge and caramel apple."

"It's made from mandala fruit," I explained. I took a bite of my peppery karbachi meat. I had often seen Marshall eating mandala bars. Personally, I didn't care for it, but humans seemed to enjoy the overwhelming sweetness. "It's tropical. Maztek is full of them."

"That's music to my ears," said Gabriella flatly. She wrinkled her nose and looked around her. "It will be the first thing I try when we get out of here. If we ever get out of here."

"We will," I assured her, tossing my empty wrapper back into the satchel. I pulled the rag over my nose and mouth again. "It's a question of when. I've never failed a mission, and I'm not about to start now," I mumbled.

"I believe you."

There was a pause in the conversation before I felt comfortable enough to ask a question that had been bothering me.

"Where did you learn to do that?"

"Do what?"

A dark shadow passed briefly over her face when she realized what I meant, but it faded quickly and her lips curled into a tight smile.

"I've had a lot of practice, I guess," said Gabriella slowly. She raised a hand to her ear and began playing with the back of her earring. "I once had to pop both my shoulder and my knee back into place when I fell from the second-floor landing. I might be related to a double-jointed superhero or something."

"Why is that? Don't humans have doctors for that kind of thing?"

"We do." Gabriella stared into space as she carefully selected her words. "You could say I've become an expert at disguising my 'accidents' over the years."

I was taking a drink of water when the implications of her words finally sunk in. Gabriella polished off the rest of her bar and crumpled the wrapper in her fists. She stopped playing with her hands and folded her fingers over her good knee. I lowered the water to my side.

"Was it your father?"

"Of course not." Gabriella's eyes were flashing. "My dad was a great man. He was a frequent visitor to Maztek. He did a lot of work there before he died in a passenger shuttle crash on his way back home. No, it was Richard. He was a drunk asshole my mother eventually married."

"And this grown man threw you out of a building?" I whispered. I kept my face blank, but I was seething inside.

"I ruined his favorite shirt when I accidentally threw my red sweater in the wash along with the whites. We were taking school pictures the next day, and I had nothing new to wear. I tossed it into the machine at the last minute without looking. Richard wasn't amused, to say the least."

I felt like an ass for assuming her life had been problem-free because she came from Earth. Like me, Gabriella was forced to mature at an early age. I realized there was an ugly side to humanity, just like everywhere else in the galaxy.

"It feels weird talking about him," Gabriella continued. She picked at the dirt under her fingernails. "I think this is the first time I've ever admitted this to anyone. I don't want people to start feeling sorry for me."

"I do not. Seeing that you've made it, and you're sitting here in front of me right now...that speaks for itself."

"Thanks."

"If it counts for anything, your father sounds like a wonderful man."

"He was. I miss him every day." The corners of her eyes drooped as she smiled sadly. She blinked and turned her gaze to me. "That's enough about me. What about you? Are you a high-up commander of the Maztek army, or something?"

I grabbed the sturdiest branch in the vicinity and took out some tools.

"My actual title is long, complicated and doesn't mean anything. My men refer to me as the General. It's the most senior position in the Maztek forces. I have a particular team. They're the ones who accompanied me on this mission. I don't like to talk about it, but I'm ultimately responsible for the thousands of troops under my command."

"No way. Are you serious?" Gabriella stammered. Her jaw dropped open. She narrowed her eyes and studied me carefully. "Well, you don't seem to be much of a prankster. Don't get me wrong, that is very impressive, but I feel ashamed right now. I was just going to brag about managing a group of five people."

"Don't sell yourself short. It isn't about the number of people. It's about being able to think about something other than your interests. Not everyone's cut out to lead."

"When you put it that way, I think you might be right," said Gabriella thoughtfully. She flattened the sides of her shiny hair and placed the gas mask back over her head. "But why the military?"

"What do you mean? What else is there?"

"Why not start a business or go into something sports-related? You don't have to kill people for a living."

"Ah," I nodded, understanding. "Well, my father, and my Upa — that's my grandfather — were both high-ranking officers. They were in the army all their lives. They were the roughest pair of individuals you could ever meet. They raised me as best they could when my mother disappeared, but died twenty years ago in the worst Xylo attack in history. It was an unprovoked strike on Fallgold, the Maztek capital. Nearly two thousand innocent children and civilians died that day. We don't even have a name for it. We just call it the Fallgold incident. Upa and my father were some of the casualties. I suppose you could say I've felt compelled to fill in their shoes since then."

"You must have been a boy back then. I'm sorry," choked Gabriella. "I don't know what to say."

"Don't be. You didn't have anything to do with it unless you were a Xylo commander in your youth. I was just answering your question."

"What could the Xylo possibly have against the Maztek? From the stories my Dad used to tell me about the planet, it seems like a peaceful place."

"You better strap in for that epic tale." My eyebrows knitted together as I stroked my beard thoughtfully. "It's a long story, but here's the abbreviated version. The Xylo are our ancestors. Centuries ago, we fled from Xylox. At the time, it was led by a tyrant named Vladimir. We escaped to an uninhabited planet now known as Maztek and rebuilt it for ourselves. We are a democratic monarchy, headed by King Jacquim, one of the finest leaders the galaxy has ever seen. As you know, this planet isn't in the best condition. The Xylos have been fighting to claim Maztek for themselves and relocate to a better world. As for Synic, his father, Dyron, died in the Fallgold incident. He's been out for revenge ever since."

"That's a shame, but I'm finding it hard to sympathize with that heartless bastard. What the fuck was that?"

A needle-nosed fly squeezed into the gap between Gabriella's ill-fitting mask and her face. She fell to the ground and started rolling around, violently swatting the air around her. I threw the branch and my tools onto the ground. Pouncing on top of her, I forced my legs around her body to stop her from moving.

"Can you get my mask off? I can feel something crawling on me!"

I yanked the gas mask away from her face. Her dilated irises focused on the fly climbing the side of her left cheek. I closed my fist and pressed it against her nose, allowing the insect to climb on my hand. But as I pivoted toward the ground, ready to release it, the little asshole went rogue. It flapped its metallic blue wings and launched itself right in my face.

"Shit!"

I dove out of its way and fell to the ground next to Gabriella. The tip of my nose was inches from hers. Her blue eyes were hypnotizing up close. I looked at the soft pink of her full lips, and my cock stirred at the strange tightening in my chest.

I sat up quickly and pushed myself off the ground.

"It's not getting any earlier," I shouted, clearing my throat. I handed her the makeshift cane I fabricated from the branch and began to repack my satchel.

"Let's move."

CHAPTER 10

GABRIELLA

We had made our way into the city, which meant I would finally get to sleep in a bed again. That is, if we could figure out how to get inside.

Laz rammed his body into the door one more time. It finally gave in and creaked open. He stepped over the threshold and pulled a rusted chain hanging by the doorway. The solitary light bulb filled the tiny room with a pitiful orange glow.

I removed my gas mask to get a better look at the place, but regretted my decision immediately. The aroma was so powerful that my eyes started watering. I held my breath and clutched the mask to my chest as I followed Lax inside. I thought the budget motels back on Earth were bad, but this place was a nightmare.

It looked like the previous tenants had trashed the hotel room decades ago and the staff had never cleaned it up. There was a fist-sized hole in the dirty window. The tiles seemed as if they might have been cream-colored in the beginning, but dirty shoe marks and suspicious stains covered them now. A monitor hung on the wall at an awkward tilt. Someone had shattered the screen a long time ago. Loose cables and wires were coming out of the back. A small door was open, leading to an unlit bathroom, but I was not brave enough to explore it.

Laz seemed unshaken by the unkempt appearance of the room. He dusted off a wooden chair and put his bag on it. I was wary of moving from my spot by the doorway. For the first time since my crash on the planet, I was grateful all my luggage had gotten lost.

"This is...rustic."

I didn't want to come off as whiny, but surely we could have afforded something better than this? My disappointment must have been visible on my face.

"This place is a piece of shit," said Laz bluntly. "We need to lay low and avoid detection from Synic and his troops."

"I guess you're right. We certainly don't want to be discovered," I agreed.

Laz took out a blue steel can he had purchased from a small corner shop. Popping off the lid, he pushed down on a nozzle and sprayed down every surface of the room. The crystal-white mist instantly cleared the stench from the air. Bubbles formed on the walls and floors, turning them a shade lighter. The room still looked old and grungy, but it was more livable than before.

Laz tossed me an extra can. I caught it and went to work on the second bed, located on the left of the nightstand. This room was the last twin suite in the building. I pinched the edges of the faded salmon covers and pulled them up to spray underneath.

"The rest of the brides...they're okay, aren't they?"

"As long as they're with my men, they are in good hands."

"I didn't mean anything by it," I assured him. Fluffing the sanitized pillow, I shuffled over to the next bed. I aimed the can at the filthy covers.

"I met a girl, Cheyenne, on the shuttle. I was wondering what happened to her."

When I looked carefully at the covers, I dropped my can and took a giant step back.

"Laz? Is this normal?"

I shook my head in disgust and denial. One hand flew to my mouth as the other began vigorously poking Laz's waist. My lips were still moving as I called out for Laz's attention, but sounds weren't making it out from my body.

"Can't you see I've got my hands full here? What now?"

Laz was shocked at the sight of the moving mattress, which seemed to be alive. The middle of the bed had a large hole in it. Within the crater was a swarming pit of tangled worms, maggots, and insects. The bundle of bugs looked like they were pulsing in the center of the bed. They were beating as one entity.

My voice finally came back to me. "What the fuck is that?!" I flung myself to the other side of the room and pressed myself flat against the wall. The room echoed with every single cuss word I knew streaming nonstop out of my mouth.

As usual, Laz moved like lighting under pressure. He clenched his teeth and reached for the mattress, gently easing it onto the floor. The only way he could get that thing out of there was to drag it across the room. Otherwise, the slimy bottom of the mattress might break through and spill its contents.

I sprinted to the front door and held it open. Laz maneuvered the mattress past me and out of the doorway. I closed one eye but left the other cracked open as he flipped the mattress over the edge of the sixth-floor railing. The mattress plunged soundlessly to the ground underneath us.

"I'm pretty sure that's one of the most disgusting things I've ever seen in my life."

"If that's true, you've led a good life. That was only a mild infestation," said Laz. A small smile crept across his lips as he closed the door behind him. "There should be some running water in the bathroom if you want to take a shower. The water starts off brown, but it will clear up if you let it run for a minute."

"I'll take what I can get. No peeking."

Laz handed me a plastic bottle filled with soap.

"Thanks."

With my expectations at an all-time low after the mattress disaster, the bathroom wasn't as bad as I had imagined. As it turned out, there was no hot water, but the force of the shower head made up for it. I was just happy I could finally wash my bra and panties. After toweling myself dry and slipping back into my tattered dress, I returned to the bedroom.

"What are we doing next?"

I fell silent when I heard the deep, leveled breathing. Laz had laid out the spare covers on the floor at the foot of the bed and was sprawled on top of it, snoring. He had his back turned to me and was facing the door. It looked like he had fallen asleep as soon as I entered the shower. I could imagine why. He had slept less than seven hours in the last three days.

I tiptoed to the bed and pulled down the covers, an extra-silky sanitizing sheet protecting my lumpy pillow and blanket. I peeked over at Laz's sleeping figure. His strong back wrinkled as he shifted his arm in his sleep.

Moving as lightly as I could, I removed the second sheet from under the covers, danced around Laz, and draped the sheet over his sleeping frame. After turning off the light, I crawled into bed quietly.

I passed out as soon as my head hit the pillow.

* * * *

Laz and I were in a dusty old freight elevator with expanding gates made from aged reinforced steel. It was big enough to house two grand pianos with room to spare. The large elevator jumped once and started moving down. I reached for the safety handle dangling above me and held onto it tightly.

"Stay close to me and don't say a word. The Xylo here will keep to themselves as long as we stay out of their way. And whatever you do, don't make eye contact with anyone."

Laz tugged on the hood of his cloak and motioned for me to adjust mine as well.

"Yes commander," I said, humoring him. I released the handle and started tucking loose strands of hair inside my hood. "What is this place, anyway?"

"I'd advise you to hold on to something."

I took his advice to heart the moment the elevator started moving *sideways*. The free-moving room careened to my left. I wasn't expecting the shift, and I flew into Laz, who grabbed me by one arm and helped me stay on my feet. I noticed there was nothing but jet-black shadows beyond the latticed gaps in the gate. The smell of sulfur mixed with gasoline permeated the musty underground atmosphere.

The elevator came to an abrupt halt less than a minute later. Laz reached for a bronze crank gleaming in the darkness and turned it counter-clockwise. The old gate slowly retracted.

"This is Bhima-Saraza," Laz said in a low voice. We stepped out of the elevator into a corridor lit with torches. "This underground marketplace is run by Xylo rebels. They're outcasts who regularly fight back against the tyrannical regime. Even though they are the enemies of our enemies, these folks are not our friends. We have to stay vigilant. Remember, at the end of the day, they are still Xylo."

"A marketplace? Sounds terrific. I'm going to need some clean clothes to wear," I piped up. The day was looking better already. My smile faded when I realized I didn't have any money. "Would you mind spotting me for now? I lost everything in the crash, and I'm not going to see any TerraMates money for a long time."

"Of course. I'll cover you." Laz cut through my babbling. He held a hand to his lips as we approached an entrance covered with a curtain. "But we can't stay here for long. I need to get parts for my communicator. Random raids by Xylo cops frequently occur in Bhima-Saraza. Make it quick."

Laz held open the curtain to let me through. I ducked under his arm and slipped through the gap. As soon as I got to the other side, I grabbed the edges of my hood in amazement.

It was not the typical open-air market I was used to back on Earth. The marketplace seemed to stretch on endlessly but I could see thick, windowless clay walls in the distance. Robust two-story clay storefronts stood along the sides of a maze of booths. It was like we had discovered a hidden underground city.

"Come on. This way," said Laz abruptly.

I always found it difficult to keep up with his long strides. As we cut our way through the aisles surrounding the stalls, my eyes looked around. I wanted to take in the fantastic scenery around me. There were Xylo men and women of all ages hustling around. Dark canopy roofs cast shadows over all the stalls despite the lack of direct sunlight.

In the booth on my right, a young Xylo man with an eye patch and blue, sinewy veins protruding out from the back of his head argued with a shopkeeper. He gesticulated with a brass trumpet and switchblade to emphasize his point. The shopkeeper, an elderly Xylo woman with a face full of tattoos, held her ground.

As we walked further along the aisle, I snuck a peek to my left. Several injured and maimed Xylo with stone-faced expressions lined up next to a booth. Behind the stall, a pair of spectacled aliens in frayed lab coats attended a patient. The ailing Xylo sat on a reclined chair. He growled and winced as the black-market doctors treated a glowing boil on his forehead with gleaming scalpels and other surgical tools. I didn't want to see an illegal operation. I turned away from the ghastly view.

Laz purchased three sets of silver and black jumpsuits and a pair of ugly black boots for me before we went on our way. He found a practically bottomless knapsack for me just like his satchel, but this one was brown suede. I gleefully packed my clothes into my new bag and swung it over my shoulder.

We reached the end of the aisle and made a turn at the end. Two Xylo children on hovering discs floated into our paths. I smiled as I went by two boys fencing with each other using painted branches. Their light and carefree laughter joined the noisy chatter of the marketplace.

The purity of their joy was refreshing. It was the first cheery sight I had seen since arriving on the planet.

I followed Laz into a rundown storefront. Not sure what to expect, I crinkled my nose and prepared myself for anything. I had to duck down under the broken signs blocking half of the doorway.

"All right, here we are. Try not to stare at anything."

"I won't." Even as the words left my mouth, I knew I was making a promise I couldn't keep. As soon as I entered the shop a vague sense of claustrophobia began to creep over me. The workshop-slash-junkyard seemed smaller than it looked from the outside because it was so cramped. The interior reminded me of an underground coal mine. I could hardly see the walls because messy mountains of machinery parts covered them. Loose pieces of equipment were stacked from floor to ceiling.

There were people in the workshop as well. Xylo staff hunched over their workstations. Some whacked away at their projects with hammers. Others leaned back from the dangerous sparks showering them from welding torches. A few peered through large magnifying lenses as they worked on miniature chips that were smaller than the tip of my pinkie. Though they appeared to be elderly, none of them looked like people you wanted hunting you.

"Do I smell a *human*?" a thunderous voice boomed from above. Startled, I jumped back and tilted my head, seeing a circular hatch in the ceiling. A long pole ran through the middle of the door, connecting the two floors.

"I'm sure I smell your blood. Who goes there?"

The workers lifted their heads and started snapping at us.

"It's me, Ryzz. Cut the crap and get your wrinkled old ass down here. I don't have another second to waste."

A rainbow blur came sliding down the pole. I blinked at the two-foot-tall Xylo, who came limping toward us with a cane. The eccentric alien looked far older than anyone in the room. I didn't know the typical Xylo life span, but if I had to guess, he looked like he had lived through a century or two. The alien wore thick goggles over his beady eyes and decorated himself with a flashy rainbow cloak adorned with bottle-cap medallions and metal trinkets.

"General Lazarus," Ryzz barked. There was a sharp tone in the deep voice that didn't seem to match his small stature. He peered up at Laz, curling his lip. "I see you still refuse to get a haircut. What brings you here, boy?"

"I need a spare Morse board for my communicator." Laz took out the device from his pocket. He handed it over to Ryzz, who leaned in for a closer look. "You got one laying around?"

"Aye."

"How much do you want for it?"

"I suppose I can part with one for seven hundred fifty credits."

"Seven hundred fifty?" Laz repeated, snorting. He crossed his arms and spread his legs apart. "For that price, I hope it's dipped in gold. Why don't you hold a gun to my head while you're at it? I didn't realize you were a thief, old man."

"Where else are you going to find such a rare part? It seems you're on the clock, too." An oily smile spread across his thin white lips. "It's nothing personal. It's just business. I have to make a living too, you know."

When Ryzz's eyes settled on me, his smile broadened. "And who do we have here? You must be the human. You know, if you're looking for a discount, we could forget credits altogether. There are alternative forms of payment. Give me a few minutes with her in the back."

"Laz!" I cried out, slapping a hand over my mouth.

Before Ryzz could complete his thought, Laz had whipped out a gun. He jammed the end of the long barrel into the Xylo's lips and turned off the safety. Ryzz's expression stayed fixed on his face, but he raised his hands in surrender. The whole workshop was paying attention to our corner of the room. We watched as Laz leaned over to whisper in Ryzz's ear. His voice was quiet, but I knew everyone could hear each word he said.

"Stand the fuck down. If you so much as look at her again, I'll blow your brains out, no questions asked. I'll pay in credits."

Laz withdrew his weapon but left it out, positioned against his hip. Ryzz signaled to one of his workers and yelled out a complicated item code. The worker returned minutes later with a black microchip wrapped in transparent film and thrust it into Laz's hands.

"Let's make this quick, and then we never have to think about each other ever again."

As Ryzz was about to answer, a deafening crash outside the workshop entrance ripped through the chatter. I took a look out the window. A team of Xylo cops in black uniforms and badges stormed through a smoking hole they created in the wall. I wondered why doors existed on this planet. Shoppers and storekeepers dispersed in all directions, running away from the cops who were wielding batons and firing random gunshots into the air. Classy.

"Move workstation four!" Ryzz boomed to his worker. He turned towards Laz and pointed with his cane. "Just go. And don't ever let me see your face around here again."

"You take care too, Ryzz."

Laz hurried me through a small ventilation shaft hidden in the wall behind the workstation. We made our way down the narrow tunnel for a few minutes before a ladder appeared in front of us. By this time, my knees were scraped raw, and my palms throbbed with pain. I gritted my teeth and pulled myself up the sticky ladder. Laz climbed behind me and helped boost me out of the escape hatch.

"Halt! Present your identification."

We turned around and found ourselves face-to-face with a floating robot shaped like a box, and fitted with yellow sirens on both sides. Laz threw a hand over me and took a step back cautiously. He put his fingers to his lips.

"Without identification, the penalty is death. Present identification in 3...2..."

"Run!"

Laz shoved me forward to give me a head start. Behind me, the drone whirred as a twin-headed barrel emerged from its top. Fiery bullets sprayed from the barrel in our general direction.

We sprinted down to the end of the street. Seeing an open manhole in front of us, we leaped down into a black void.

CHAPTER 11

LAZ

As we plummeted into the darkness, I desperately looped an arm around the first thing I saw - a glint of metal. I clung to the side of the pipe and hauled Gabriella close to me with an outstretched arm. She was petite, but the stiffness of her frozen arms and legs made it seem like she weighed more than she did. I swung my leg over the top of the pipe and secured her in front of me.

"Sit up straight and keep your hands on both sides so you don't fall off."

"Thanks, like I didn't know that already," Gabriella snapped. She trembled as she looked over at me and shot me a blistering glance. At least the shaking meant she was able to move again. "Hurry up with whatever you're doing back there. I can feel my hands starting to slip."

I ignored Gabriella's hysterical cries and took out the only light source I had left. The cylinders were small enough to keep in my pocket, but they only lasted about half an hour. I twisted it open and activated the light.

"Just hold on a little longer."

I took out a grappling hook and extendable rope, tying a knot in the center of the claw. Securing the line, I attached the end of the rope to my belt loop. I pulled both ends to make sure it was secure.

"I don't have a choice if I want to stay alive. Can you just get me down from here? Please?"

I pulled Gabriella close to me and placed her arms on my shoulders. She was swinging dangerously, and she couldn't stop looking at the depths underneath us. Her icy fingers trembled as they tightened around my neck. As soon as the hook was anchored, I held her chin in my hand.

"You can do this. Don't look down. Trust me."

Gabriella nodded weakly. Holding her in front of me, I carefully released my legs from the sides of the pipe. We smoothly slid down with the assistance of the extendable rope. I held out my light to guide the path. When we approached the ground, I adjusted our descent and moved to the side. We touched down on the landing next to a flowing passage of sewer sludge.

She lifted her new satchel and bent down. With her hands cupped over her kneecaps, she fought to catch her breath. I reached over to take her bag and stepped back to give her some room.

"Do you need some water?"

She didn't answer for a minute. "No, I'll be all right, thank you," Gabriella replied, panting. She straightened her back and took her satchel back. "I'm sorry for barking at you like that. Heights and I don't mix."

"I gathered as much," I quickly said as I turned my head away. "If you can move, we should get out of here. I don't know how much longer this light is going to last. Are you ready?"

"I'm good enough to go," said Gabriella. She removed her gas mask from the satchel and placed it over her head. "Let's do it."

Even though the Xylox sewage system smelled like excrement and death, it was less toxic than the air above ground. There were different dangers in the sewers. Discolored water constantly dripped from the leaky overhead pipes. Damp rats with crooked spines and shrunken heads were everywhere. They weren't afraid of us. Instead, they looked up at us curiously with glowing red eyes as they scurried over our boots.

I knew Gabriella remained tense behind me, but she was a good soldier. Her desire to get out of here made her move faster than before. We headed east and forged ahead until we saw a sliver of light coming from a loose manhole cover above us. I shined the light around, revealing a set of steps bolted to the wall.

"Here we go."

I shoved the light into Gabriella's hand and pulled out the pouch containing my communicator pieces. Gabriella crouched next to me and shined the blinking light on my hands. I tore off the seal to the Morse board with my teeth and started reassembling the communicator. But as I squinted at the electronics in front of me, I realized there was a problem.

"Damn it!" My angry cry echoed through the tunnel.

"What's wrong?" asked Gabriella softly. She removed her mask and blankly stared at the communicator in my hands. "Are you missing something?"

"One of the pins must have snapped off when this thing fell apart," I grumbled. I kicked a piece of gravel to my left. The rock briefly floated on the sludge before it started to smoke and disappeared below the dark surface. Next to me, Gabriella began to fiddle with her right ear. She removed an earring and held it out to me in the palm of her hands.

I pinched the post of the small diamond earring between my fingers and examined it carefully.

"This might work." My forehead wrinkled as I gazed at her intently. "Are you sure you're okay with letting me use this? I'm going to have to break it apart. Is it a family heirloom?"

"It's fine," said Gabriella, waving a hand. "I'm not concerned with having matching earrings right now, if you know what I mean."

"Your sacrifice will be long remembered by the Maztek."

I twisted off the diamond and slipped it into my chest pocket. The repair would require delicate precision and a steady hand. I pushed the gold earring post against the resistor and manipulated the earring back on its side to hold the resistor in place. As soon as I heard a gratifying click, I puffed out my chest and beat my thigh twice with my fist. It was a silent and watered-down version of a Maztek victory bellow.

"Was that good?"

"It means I've set it in place. Half the screen has been shattered, so now we're going to find out if this thing even works."

I turned a knob on the communicator and adjusted it from side to side. The green light on the top of the screen blinked, giving me hope. Gabriella cheered enthusiastically over my shoulder. But when a deep crackling came out of the speaker, I groaned.

"There's no signal down here. I'm going to have to climb to the top. Stay close to me, and don't move any further unless I tell you to. Understood?"

"Yes, commander," Gabriella mumbled. She rose from the ground and looked me in the eye. "Lighten up a little. You can live life without everything being an order."

I stared at her for a moment but swallowed my snippy retort.

"While we're down here, give me a second to change out of these nasty clothes."

"You have two minutes."

I aimed the light toward her body and turned away to face the opposite wall. Gabriella shimmied out of her torn dress. She rolled it into a ball and casually tossed it into the sewer sludge. I could hear a soft unzipping behind me, and I couldn't control my thoughts. I knew she was naked and she would look fantastic.

My eyes focused on the distinct shadow of her body cast against the wall. The side view of her silhouette showed off the rounded curve of her breasts contrasted against her flat stomach. Her hourglass figure bent forward. As she rolled the pants of her jumpsuit over her leg, the shadow of her jiggling breasts shook along with her body. The lustful sight was enough to bring my cock to attention. I averted my eyes and relocated them to a smudge on my boot.

"I'm all set now."

I turned around. All my years spent playing cards were put to good use when I made eye contact with her without revealing my thoughts. She looked good enough to devour in her skintight black jumpsuit. The zipper which ran down the middle of the suit was open over her chest. Seeing the globes of her perky breasts made me want to reach out and touch them.

She ran a hand through her hair and shook it loose over her shoulders. I turned away, ostensibly to investigate the manhole steps but secretly to adjust the sudden tightness in my crotch.

Gabriella handed me a fresh rag for my face before putting her gas mask on again. I grunted at her in appreciation and tied it over my head. With Gabriella behind me, I moved up the cold steps and scaled the length of the wall. I stopped before the manhole opening and held the communicator to my ear.

"Hold."

The crackling continued. Either we weren't high enough, or the cover itself was interfering with the transmission. I reached out and pushed off the cover with the tips of my fingers. The thick metal disc made a loud noise when I moved it aside. I climbed to the top and lifted Gabriella out of the hole by the waist, setting her down next to me.

I was still squatting when the crackling subsided. I distinctly heard a beep from the device before the faint sounds of scrambled voices started to come over the communicator. As I tinkered some more, trying to make the voices even clearer, Gabriella began to poke at my side with her finger. Anger flooded my mind. I needed to concentrate. I turned around to face her.

"What are you doing?"

"Behind you, Laz – watch out!"

I had been so immersed in getting the communicator to work that I had completely missed a figure waddling toward us. Gabriella jumped to her feet and clumsily swung her fist over my head. The figure lifted her off the ground instantly and flung her aside. Gabriella's airborne body hit a crooked street pole before falling limply to the ground.

A Xylo security officer wearing tinted red goggles beat his chest with gloved fists. He seemed pretty excited for taking down a girl. I bounced off the ground and sprang on top of him before he could draw his holstered weapon. We crashed to the dirt, rolling around as we wrestled for his pistol.

More adrenaline pumped into my system. I managed to get my hand on the weapon on the other side of his belt. Slipping my fingers over the trigger, I pulled back, aimed, and fired in a single motion. An electric charge shot from the mouth of the gun and incapacitated him. The Xylo convulsed briefly before his arms and legs became immobilized, and he fell over on his side.

Turning on my heel, I vaulted toward Gabriella. She lay unconscious by the base of the dented street pole. I lifted the side of her head and laid it in my lap. There was a small gash over her eyebrow, but there were no other visible signs of injury. I pressed two fingers against her neck. Feeling her faint but steady pulse beating against my fingertips, I let out a breath I didn't know I had been holding.

I heard shouting behind me. My neck creaked as I looked over my shoulder. Either the Xylo weapon was undercharged, or the security officer weighed too much for the shock to knock him out for long. The Xylo was regaining sensation in his limbs. He snaked his way across the asphalt, rolling on his greasy stomach and heading toward his hover bike, which was still running. It was on standby a few inches off the ground.

I hooked Gabriella's satchel over my shoulder. Scooping her off the ground, I carried her to the hover bike and carefully positioned her in the seat. The security officer tried to pull me off his bike, but he was still crawling around on the ground. I trampled over his fingers. The sickening crunch of breaking bones mixed with his agonizing screams in the air.

Grabbing the keys from his belt, I secured Gabriella before mounting the hover bike myself. Black smog coughed out of the tailpipe as the bike lifted off the ground, blowing in the Xylo's unconscious face.

CHAPTER 12

GABRIELLA

The wooden planks of the bridge sunk slightly under my weight. I wavered and held onto the railing. In the sunlight, it almost looked like the bridge glowed a pristine white. I wondered if I was leaving tracks with my muddy shoes. When I looked behind me, there wasn't a spot in sight.

I did a double-take when I wiggled my toes.

The sky-blue ballet flats Dad gave me years ago sparkled on my feet. But they couldn't have been the same pair. The ones he got fit me when I was a child, but the shoes I was wearing were perfect for my adult body. I also remembered Richard throwing them out when I had accidentally spilled paint on the dining table. I raised one of my legs and tilted my head to the side. The hand-stitched sequins, the little white bows – the shoes were nearly identical.

Shrugging, I proceeded to the other end of the bridge. I didn't have a clue about my location but there was a strong sense of familiarity. I had been here before. Bushes with blue and violet flowers grew along the sides of the clear water. The grass tickled my feet as I walked across it.

I followed the trail of a winding stone path. Wooden signs with unintelligible blood-red symbols poked out of the grass by the sidelines. When I reached the end of the road, I noticed my toes were tingling. It felt like my ballet flats had a mind of their own.

I left the trail and walked across the slope of a small hill.

"How are you doing, Shooting Star?"

My heart did a little flip in my chest. I slowly turned to the man sitting on the grass a few feet away from me. A soft touch of gray peppered his carefully parted hair. The only other hints of his age were bags under his eyes. He had a terribly handsome face. A pair of gold-rimmed frames sat on the bridge of his nose. His glasses were slightly lopsided on the right side, supported by an uneven ear. The initials "K.M.H," were printed on the pocket of his tailored brown coat.

"Dad?"

"Of course." Wrinkles formed next to his eyes as he beamed at me. He patted the patch of ground next to him. "Let's chat."

I joined him on the grass, hugging my legs. "Am I dead?"

Dad held his stomach and threw his head back. His uninhibited laughter rang across the sweeping landscape. I rested my cheek against my knee and watched him, smiling.

"Don't be silly, Gabriella. Of course not."

"What am I doing here, then?"

"I don't know," said Dad. He winked. "You tell me."

"Beats me."

He raised an eyebrow. "Is that all you have to say to me after so long apart?"

"Where are we?"

"Why don't you take a look around and see if you can figure it out for yourself?"

I sat up and looked at the beautiful water in front of me. A paddle leaned against the wooden dinghy docked by the river bank. Beyond that stood a quaint country cottage with a thick black roof that looked like a mushroom cap. My eyes lit up when it hit me.

"I'm at the lake behind Grandma Molly's house," I breathed dreamily. My chin quivered. "You taught me how to ride a bike on that stone path when I was six. I felt awful when I heard Grandma Molly sold the cottage."

"I was sad to hear the news, too," Dad shared ruefully. He looked on at the cottage and whistled. "I had a lot of great memories here. All those girls I brought back to my room when I was a teenager..."

"Stop right there." I held a hand up to his face, smiling behind my groan. "Too much. Not ready to hear that, and don't think I ever will be."

"Fair enough." Dad was still chuckling. His smile slowly faded. "How have you been holding up, kiddo?"

"Where do I start?" I sighed dramatically. My throat was beginning to feel thick. I tried to kick things off on a lighter note. "I think Mom's around your age now. I saw her a couple of weeks ago. You've aged far better than she has, if that means anything to you."

"Maybe a little," said Dad. His eyes twinkled.

"You know, I thought I wouldn't be able to control myself when I saw her. But I wasn't angry anymore. I felt pity for how old and unhealthy she is, but it felt like encountering a stranger at a bus stop."

"I can understand that." Dad's voice was gentle and brooding. "Gabriella, I'm sorry about everything you had to go through. I wasn't there for you, Shooting Star."

"Sorry?" My words sounded distant and forced. "It wasn't your fault. You weren't an abusive drunk who beat his wife into submission and went crazy when he couldn't do the same thing with his stepdaughter."

"You know I would never let anything happen to you if I was around."

"I know, I know," I groaned. I buried my face in my hands. "I'm lashing out for no reason now, and it isn't fair to you, so I'll stop."

"You're angry."

"No kidding." My voice dripped sarcasm. "Considering everything that's happened so far? I wonder why that would be."

"Gabriella, I know this is hard for you, but you're going to have to learn to stop keeping all your anger in a little ball inside you. You need to let things go."

"That's easy for you to say," I retorted. "You're dead. You're done with all the bullshit. You're not the one who was left alone to navigate through life all by herself."

"I'm sorry, Shooting Star."

I leaned my head against Dad's shoulder. The physical contact was more than I could handle and I felt tears start to fall. I slipped my arm under his and clung to his body. He seemed solid to me. If I closed my eyes and concentrated hard enough, I could almost smell his particular scent: peppermint and traces of cologne.

"I'm sorry, Dad." I could barely see him anymore through my tears. "I miss you."

"I know," he whispered. He petted my head and planted a kiss on my forehead. "I miss you more."

"How do you always stay so happy, Dad?" I tilted my head to look up at him. "No offense, but why aren't you bitter and resentful like anyone else would be? Do you know what was happening back home all the times you were away at Maztek? Do you have any idea how many strange men have been in your room?"

"I've always known," he admitted glumly. "Your mother's weak. I made my peace with that years ago. If I had done anything about it, they would have taken you away from me."

I wouldn't let it go. "But you've worked so hard all your life only to die in your prime." I wasn't convinced. "I don't mean to sound like I'm accusing you of anything. But some answers would be nice."

"You might not always find answers, honey, but there's a reason for everything."

"What does that even mean? That's too philosophical. I need straight talk."

"Just trust your gut, Gabriella. You were born with instincts for a reason. I'm proud of you, Shooting Star. You're everything I've hoped you would turn out to be. Everything is going to be just fine – I promise."

I stood up immediately. I didn't like the tone of Dad's words.

"You're not leaving, are you?"

"I'm not going anywhere. They're telling me it's time for you to go."

"I don't *want* to go."

"I know, honey. I know."

Quiet tears poured down my cheeks. They soaked into Dad's pants as I rested my head in his lap. Dad pulled the lapel of his coat and took out his mandolin. I had not seen the gorgeous wooden instrument in years.

The sides of the pure black wood had a painted scene of musical notes flying through the cosmos. The largest shooting star had the word "Gabriella" painted across it.

I huddled close to him. I wanted to make this moment last as long as possible. My eyes squeezed shut as I relished every gentle pluck of the mandolin strings.

Beyond the four stars, with the whispers of this melody

I carry this heart forever, my naima, you'll be.

* * * *

"Gabriella?"

I groaned. A pair of strong hands grabbed me by the shoulders and shook me incessantly.

"Gabriella? Can you hear me?"

"I have a headache."

My head was in splitting pain. I had to open my eyes as slowly as possible. Adjusting to the light shining on my face added to my headache. I felt horrible. There wasn't an inch of my body that didn't hurt.

My legs were spread open. I tried lifting my right leg to close them, but the severe stiffness overtaking my muscles told me I should give myself a chance to rest.

I blinked rapidly. My eyes drifted to the hands holding my shoulders up. As soon as the blurriness subsided, I remembered. It felt like I saw the four black asterisks

129

tattooed onto Laz's knuckles for the first time. He leaned over and gently lowered my head back onto my pillow.

"Four stars," I rasped groggily. I winced. My parched throat burned every time I tried to speak.

"What was that? Did you say something? **Can you hear me?**"

"Will you please," I gasped. My eyebrows snapped together as my eyes fell back shut. "Keep it down."

I heard Laz exhale and fall to the ground. One of my eyes curiously opened. Laz was on the floor of our room. His hands were on his face with his fingers pressed against his temples. A thin sheen of sweat covered all the tension points on his body – his forehead, chest, and under his armpits. The expression of concern was something I hadn't seen from him before. I didn't think I had ever seen him show emotions other than annoyance and anger.

"Can I get some water?"

Laz stood up and pulled out a bottle of water from my knapsack. He opened it with one hand and held the back of my head with the other. I lifted my chin and greedily swallowed the water he poured into my mouth. The cold drink brought life back into my strained vocal chords.

"Thanks." I licked my lips and fluffed my pillow against the shaky headboard.

"How are you feeling? Try lifting your arms and wiggling your toes."

I wanted to move, but it was difficult. Lances of pain shot down my back whenever I tried to lift a finger. It was nearly unbearable. Laz knelt next to the bed and reached for my hand.

Color swept across my cheeks. My palms started to tingle. I shifted on the bed and lay against my pillow. Laz pried apart my thumb and index finger and massaged the swollen pressure point. He only touched my hand, but I thought I could feel my pulse rate increasing from his touch.

"Whatever it is you're doing, it's working." My low moans of pleasure filled the silence. "My head feels lighter already."

"Good."

"What happened? Did you get him? Ow!"

Laz dropped my hand abruptly. He got to his feet and loomed over me with his arms folded across his chest. I rubbed the sore spot on my elbow, glaring at him.

"What's your problem?"

"I've had it with you and your inability to follow simple orders."

"If you say 'orders' one more time, I'm going to go crazy." I threw up my hands halfway in frustration. "Ow! Damn it."

"I don't know how they do things back on Earth, but take a look around." Laz gestured wildly with his arms as he lectured me. "You're going to have to adjust your feelings. You're on Xylox, for fuck's sake. If you don't do what I tell you to do, you're going to die out here. End of story."

"That's rich, coming from you," I fired back. My rising anger was temporarily numbing the pain in my body. I wasn't ready to back down. "I'm pretty sure I saved your ungrateful butt out there."

"I'm the one with over twenty years of training under his belt. Not you."

"If that's your version of a 'thank you,' let me be the first to tell you, mister – it sucks."

Laz stared at me for a moment. He was so angry I thought steam might shoot out of his nostrils. His chest suddenly deflated. He relaxed his hands, which had curled into fists, and snatched his bag from the floor.

"Going somewhere? Why am I not surprised?"

"I'm going to find some specialized tools. My communicator broke when that fat bastard rolled over it. I stole his communicator, but it needs to be rewired to reach my crew's frequency."

"Do you need some company?"

"No," said Laz immediately. He turned the doorknob open, unnecessarily adding, "You've helped enough for today."

"Just trying to be a good girl!" I called out resentfully to the slamming door. "Jerk."

Shaking my head, I touched the back of my hand against my cheek to calm myself down. But as I pulled off the covers to look at myself, I shook my head. I saw several nasty abrasions and bruises on my arms and legs. Laz had treated every one of them with blue ointment. I twisted my neck to look at my back. A light cloth covered the large gash running next to my spine.

I looked at my washed and folded jumpsuit sitting on the chair by the wall. On my nightstand was a mug of soup. It was still hot enough to drink.

I felt a sting of guilt for my last remark.

CHAPTER 13

LAZ

As I lifted the small bag of tools from the counter, I made sure to thank the storekeeper. The old Xylo grunted in reply. He half-heartedly twirled the end of his long, wispy mustache. He pretended like he wasn't paying attention, but I knew his unblinking eyes remained fixed on me until I left his shop.

The putrid stench of the Xylox atmosphere assaulted me as soon as I stepped outside. I reached inside my hood and pulled the rag down over my face, securing it before I moved down the sidewalk.

It wasn't only the air that stunk on this planet. Only a few street lights were working. The simple action of walking down the road was enough to drain the life out of anyone. The impoverished community I saw in front of me lay in shambles, and I could only assume it was representative of the other towns on the planet.

Some buildings and formerly tall towers stood lopsided on their bases. Squatters claimed any crumbling high-rise buildings that happened to remain upright, developing distinct communities of their own. Many families, forced into homelessness because of the war effort, ended up populating the ruins of abandoned construction sites.

Now it was nighttime and children were running around unsupervised. Young, unemployed Xylo hoodlums loitered in groups on street corners, guffawing and hurling insults at passing strangers.

It was easy for an off-worlder to pick out the homes and businesses of the fortunate. The entrances to the upper-class residential and commercial structures were chained and bolted shut. The expensive areas hired private security to watch their places day in and day out.

I passed an old brown warehouse with an unusually large number of power cables and wires running through dirty windows. The warehouse was eight stories tall, but only the first four floors from the ground up were in use. Foggy purple lights and loud, obnoxious music emitted from the building. Judging from all the shifty individuals entering and leaving, I suspected it was a casino.

The warehouse was a mental landmark I used to remind myself that I was near our room. I had passed this way a few times without incident, but today a scuffling disturbance caught my attention. My Xylese vocabulary was limited, but cries of distress were universal.

The commotion came from behind me, in an alley sandwiched between two buildings constructed a little too close together. When I approached, I saw a hysterical older woman clutching onto her purse. Two Xylo men had her trapped.

I wondered if I should even get involved. Did I care if another Xylo random died? We were at war with their planet, after all. But I didn't have time to think further. In front of my eyes, the half-naked and barefoot assailants wrestled away her purse and shoved her to the ground. One slipped his hands around the stolen purse while the other held her down. Before the sick pervert could reach under the hem of the thrashing woman's dress, I sprang into action.

I noisily dropped my bag of tools. The two men turned their small black eyes in my direction. The one on the ground withdrew his hand from the screaming woman's legs but stayed sitting on her ankles, which prevented her from running away. The second Xylo with gold hoops on his ears tilted his head to one side and started inching toward me.

Were they brothers? They looked similar, and I couldn't imagine anyone voluntarily partnering with one of these losers. Pierced Ears barked at me and pointed at the woman at the ground emphatically. The skin around his mouth cracked when he grinned.

I hoped he wasn't offering me sloppy seconds.

From the corner of my eye, I could see the terror on the woman's face. Her wide eyes didn't have any tears, but her expression was distraught and hopeless.

Pierced Ears motioned to me, beckoning me closer. As he raised his hand, I strode forward and grabbed it with my fist. I yanked him toward me and twisted his arm, sending him to his knees. He howled at my feet and handed over the stolen purse without prompting. I held him by the hoops of his ear and swung him into the side of the building. The bloody earrings tore off in the scuffle and bounced across the ground.

The other creep leaped off the woman's legs, calling out to his unresponsive brother. While he was distracted, the woman crawled backward and took shelter in a corner of the dead end. The angry Xylo turned on me, wailing in despair. He looked at the ground, reached down, and grabbed a shard of broken glass. Holding it pointed away from his body, he started to charge at me.

I didn't have to think. My military-trained arm swung out instinctively and caught him by the wrist. I took a step, turned, and twisted, pinning his arm behind his back. As the thug struggled with me, I punched him in the face. His jaw dislocated with a loud popping noise. After I kicked the scrawny Xylo off his feet, I picked him up and hurled him towards the wall, next to his fallen brother.

Even though he had a severe injury on his face, the mean bastard was determined to finish the robbery. He sprang from the ground again and stalked toward the woman. I knelt down and retrieved a knife from my ankle strap. If my fists weren't enough, I would have to use a weapon.

The woman covered her face with her arms and ineffectively tried to keep her assailant at bay with an outstretched leg. I swooped in from behind him and threw my arm around his neck. I attempted to pull him off of her, but his adrenaline-induced rage made him stronger than I had anticipated. As I pushed his broken jaw and pressed my blade over his throat, his head squirmed out of my grasp. He opened his mouth, revealing two rows of jagged gray teeth that sunk into my hand.

"Fuck!" I roared. My fingers opened and dropped the blade to the ground. My skin was usually tough enough to withstand some bruising, but the sheer force of his bite penetrated my hand. Blood started to flow out of the puncture wounds and down my wrist. I tried to ignore the pain and gripped his head with both hands, jerking it forcefully to the side. His lifeless body crumpled at my feet, leaving my bloody palm print visible on his neck.

My arm was starting to glisten blue from my blood. I grunted and returned the purse. She pulled herself to her feet shakily and started bowing to me, saying something in a different language that I couldn't understand.

I waved my good hand at her. I didn't have time to talk, and I didn't want her to come up and get a good look at me. But as I backed away, I stepped on the end of my cloak. My foot pulled my hood, revealing my face. The woman took one step toward me and halted abruptly. Her pale lips opened. Now *she* started moving back as she raised a crooked finger at me.

"Don't worry," I assured her breathlessly. "Do you speak Standard? I'm not going to hurt you —"

"Halt! Present your identification."

Shit. Not again. I stopped moving, but I could see the shadow cast from the Xylo drone hovering behind me. My muscles grew tense, and I was ready to fight. But I had forgotten about the woman. Would I be able to protect her too? I took a chance and looked up, staring at her. It looked like she was trying to hide inside the wall.

"Without identification, the penalty is death. Present identification in 3..."

I saw her throat move as she swallowed. She seemed to be thinking about something, and eventually she reached into her purse, taking out a thick green card. She walked up to the drone behind me and held her card over its scanner.

"Thank you for presenting your identification."

I grabbed my things and nodded at her before staggering off in the opposite direction.

* * * *

I held my palm under the light of the motel hallway and ran my fingers over the crude stitches. Dried blood still covered my hand. The salve had sealed up part of the wound, but I had needed to finish closing the cut myself. I spread out my fingers, but when I tried to wiggle them, a sharp jab of pain flared up in my hand.

"Damn," I growled.

I heard faint giggles around me. A potbellied Xylo in a pink silk robe stumbled up the stairs. He wrapped his hairy arms around two Xylo women clutching near-empty bottles of hard liquor. I opened the door quickly and ducked into the room before they could see me.

"Finally. What took you so long? What happened to you?"

Gabriella clapped a hand over her mouth and pulled off her covers. She hobbled towards me and patted me down frantically. I took a step back from her and held out my hand for inspection. She pored over the blood stains on my cloak.

"I'm fine. It's not as bad as it looks."

Gabriella was determined to help me. She brought me some water and forced it to my lips. I gratefully chugged down the drink as she took the bag from me and set it down at her feet.

"No offense, but you look like shit. What kind of a store did you go to?"

I handed her the water and wiped my mouth with my sleeve. "It's nothing. Two Xylo thugs got in my way. One bit my hand, but I closed it up before it could hurt me."

"Are you sure you're okay? Maybe there's something I can get you, or watch over you."

"No, you've..." I bit my tongue and shook my head. "No thank you. You should get back in bed. Did you drink the medicine I left for you?"

"Yes, I did." Gabriella sank to the foot of the bed. "It's not the best thing I've ever tasted, but it's helped with the soreness. It's getting easier to move around."

"That's the idea."

I stripped off my stained clothes and tossed them onto the chair. Gabriella watched as I dumped out my treasure. A can of black spray paint rolled across the floor and stopped at a bedpost. We would use the paint later to disguise the hover bike. I needed the tools to adjust the stolen communicator so I could talk to my people.

"Listen, Laz. I've had some time to think about what happened to me. I just realized that I haven't thanked you."

"What for?"

Gabriella tucked a lock of hair behind her ear. I replaced the coupler and began the hot-wiring process.

"You know. Rescuing me. Fixing me up and everything else. You could have left me to die out there, but you didn't. Thank you. I know I've been hard to deal with for the last couple of days, but I'm truly grateful."

"Don't mention it."

"I still don't understand why you came to get me. There are plenty of other women on Earth who would be happy to marry a sexy Maztek commander. You could have gotten a refund from TerraMates."

"It's my job. This isn't my first rescue mission."

"Oh, right," Gabriella muttered quickly. She blushed and started to stammer. "Of course. That wasn't exactly what I was insinuating, but it's good to know."

"I wouldn't have left you there," I said tonelessly. I held the communicator closer to my face. Sweat was starting to accumulate on my furrowed brows from my concentration. The stitches on my palm stung. "If I ended up going to Xylox, then I ended up going to Xylox."

"That sounds...logical," Gabriella replied slowly. She couldn't sit still – she was jittery and fidgeting with her hands. "I guess I just wanted to make it clear that this isn't my usual personality. Being the damsel in distress, I mean. I've always been an independent woman."

"I don't doubt that. Fuck!"

"What's wrong?"

The pliers fell from my grasp and hit the floor with a clang. Gabriella rolled off the bed and sat next to me.

I set down the communicator and grabbed a sterilizing salve from my satchel. She took the tube from me and squeezed some onto the bleeding wound. I almost started to tell her that I could handle things myself, but I managed to hold my tongue. To be honest, I guess I didn't hate the way she tenderly dabbed ointment on my cut with her small fingers.

"You know there's nothing the matter with asking for help, right?" Gabriella reached over and grabbed the communicator and pliers from the floor. "My back is still killing me, but my hands are perfectly fine. Why don't I give it a whirl? Tell me what to do, and I'll follow your lead. I used to bead my jewelry, and I have an ex-boyfriend, so I have some experience manipulating small objects."

"We can try," I agreed after some thought. I laid my palm face up on my lap. "You have smaller hands, so it might be easier for you to twist these wires."

"Which ones need work?"

Gabriella leaned close to me and held up the communicator to my face. I couldn't help noticing that her soft breast pressed against the side of my chest. I swallowed and leaned away. She looked up at me expectantly with innocent, blue eyes.

"Hello?"

"It's complicated. Loop the thick black wire over the orange wire, then twist the green, white, and red wires together, and thread them through the second hole. Be very careful with the three wires. They're thin and solid copper, not stranded. If you break one of them, the whole thing's useless."

"I'm not feeling any pressure at all," said Gabriella, taking a deep breath. She raised her eyebrows. "It sounds simple enough. Here goes nothing."

"Take your time."

"Uh-huh." Gabriella slid the black wire under the orange one smoothly. "Now that I've got the easy part out of the way, time to twist some wires together."

She began to hum a strikingly familiar tune. I wrinkled my forehead and sat up straight, watching her carefully. As she brought the communicator close to her face, she

143

narrowed her eyes into slits and poked out her tongue from the side of her mouth.

"Is that a popular song on Earth?"

"What? Sorry, it's a weird habit of mine. I hum it sometimes when I'm concentrating. It helps me shut out all the other noises in the room. It's not a pop tune - it's just a song my dad wrote for me. He used to sing it to me all the time."

"Your father?" There was a strange flutter in my stomach. No. It couldn't be. "What was his name?"

"His first name was Keith, but everyone knew him by his second name, Marshall."

"But your father's last name is Stein, correct?"

"It's not. Hang on a second...got it." Gabriella held up the communicator triumphantly.

"Your father's last name?"

"Stein is my mother's maiden name. She had it changed after Dad died. It let her claim she was a single mom and receive payouts from the government. My Dad's last name was Hathaway. Does it matter?"

I was stunned. I hadn't moved a muscle, but I felt the floor shifting beneath me. I couldn't describe the strange feeling coursing through my body. Gabriella set down the communicator and slowly inched closer to me.

"Laz? Are you okay?"

"Your father. Marshall. Does he have a slightly protruding right ear?"

"Yes, he does. Wait a second. How would you know that?"

I found myself without the proper words to say. Except one. The only thing that came out of my mouth was the single word invading my mind.

"Naima?"

CHAPTER 14

GABRIELLA

"What did you say?"

I stared at Laz, nervously sticking my thumbs into my fists. I had never seen Laz as shaken as this before. His eyes were darting back and forth. The worry lines on his face were prominent.

How did he know these things about my father? I was bursting with questions, but I wasn't getting any answers.

"Never mind about that," Laz replied curtly. He reached for some water and tilted his head back. He drank it all in one swallow.

"It's going to be hard to get me to drop that topic of conversation. How do you know so much about my Dad? Did you do a background check on me?"

"No." Laz reached into his satchel and took out a small case. He split it open, revealing a secret compartment in the back before handing it to me. "I might have known him. Is this a picture of your father?"

I took his card holder and inspected the faded photograph on the back. There were three figures in the picture, casually posed in mid-laughter in front of a Maztek military shuttle. The handsome alien on the left appeared to be in his mid-thirties. He had wavy brown hair, and tattoos peeked out from under the rolled-up sleeves of his army fatigues. The alien in the middle was considerably older.

146

He had a silver-gray ponytail and an old scar that prevented his left eye from fully opening. Even now it looked like he could make girls swoon.

On the far right of the picture, as clear as water from the lake behind Grandma Molly's house, stood a familiar shape. It was Dad. I recognized his smile immediately. The grin that used to put me to sleep at night stretched from ear to ear.

"That's my father and Upa, next to Marshall."

"Oh my God." I traced the outline of Dad's face with the tip of my finger. A single tear rolled down my face, lingering on my chin. "How is this possible?"

"It's a long story. I might as well fix us something to eat while I think about the best way to tell it."

Laz emptied out a bag and pulled two plain brown packages out of it. He set a tray in front of me. The flimsy tray had two sections. A coin-sized lump of black dough sat on one side. The other was deeper and contained a handful of brown powder. Laz ripped open a smaller packet and poured its contents onto both ends of the tray. Within seconds, the dough fluffed up, swelling into a small loaf of bread. The brown powder started foaming and turning into a thick, questionable gravy.

"Dig in."

With one hand, I took a crunchy bite of bread, which tasted as dry and unappetizing as it looked when it was a powder. The other held the photograph. I couldn't stop looking at it.

"Is it real? If it's fake, it's not a funny joke."

"It is." Laz replied with his mouth full. He was already sopping up the gravy with the last pieces of his bread. "Marshall and my father were especially close."

"I can't believe it. I thought Earth was small, but this feels like a cosmic coincidence. What about you? Did you know my Dad personally?"

"Yes."

"Well?" I demanded, setting the mostly uneaten bread back down on my tray. "Go on, don't just stop there!"

"He was an honorable human, and would have been a fine Maztek," said Laz. He looked at me, but his eyes were unfocused, as if he were replaying memories in his head. "When my father and Upa died in battle, he always made time in his busy schedule to check on me. He helped me keep focused through my adolescent years."

"That sounds like him." I blinked back my tears and reluctantly dipped my bread into the salty gravy. "I'm a Daddy's girl, so maybe I'm biased, but he was the most generous and compassionate man I've ever known. Everyone else came before his needs. Even those who didn't deserve it."

Before now, I had never spoken a word about Dad to another living creature. Not concerned school teachers, not coworkers, and definitely not Jake. I felt my body start to relax. It felt freeing to talk about the man I immortalized and held tightly to my heart.

"There was a homeless man named Skippy that used to panhandle near my house. I don't think any of us knew his real name. I saw him sometimes on the way to school or on my way back. We never talked, but he would wave at me. I would see Dad giving him food, clothes, or money when he could. He did stuff like that all the time. I guess it was part of his character. He did what he could for other people wherever he was. One day, I stopped seeing Skippy on my way to school. Weeks went by, but he stopped showing up. I thought poverty had finally gotten to him until I ran into him at a grocery store about two years ago. He's employed as a lawyer now. I didn't even recognize him. In fact, he was the one who approached me."

"Your father gave him more than you have ever imagined." Laz finished my thought. He nodded to himself as he put the communicator back together. He screwed the sides shut and began toying with the knobs.

"He did. You probably think I cry all the time, but I don't cry much. I hadn't shed a tear for three years, but when I saw Skippy again, I lost control of myself. I got off work early that day and rushed home. Jake still hadn't moved from the couch, of course..."

"Jake? Is that the roommate you mentioned?"

"Oh, right." I tugged on my earlobe and twirled a strand of hair around my finger. "Well, yes, but not exactly. He wasn't just a roommate. We were in a relationship for almost nine years. It's more complicated than it sounds."

"I see." He didn't probe any further.

"Do you think you could tell me a story about my Dad? I would love to hear anything about him."

"No."

My mouth dropped open in protest. "But...why not?"

"You didn't let me finish. What I meant to say was – no, but I could show you, if you like."

"Show me?" I wrinkled my forehead. "What do you mean by that?"

"It's a Maztek practice we call *tawarid mana*," Laz explained, scratching the back of his neck. "Other people have done it to me a few times, but I was always on the receiving end. This will be the first time I'm sending my memories to another. You'll have to keep your expectations low, but it can't hurt to try."

"Okay." I started to push myself off the floor. "What do I have to do? Is it going to hurt?"

"Sit down. You shouldn't feel anything as long as I do it correctly."

"Okay," I shrugged. I stuck my butt on the floor again and leaned back against the side of the bed. "I trust you."

"This might sound strange, but I'm going to need to hold your hands."

I held out my hands to him obediently, hoping I wouldn't start to sweat. He looked uncomfortable as well, releasing a flustered sigh as he placed my palms flat on his. Once I saw them close together, I realized my hands looked tiny next to his. The tips of my fingers barely reached the bottom fold line of his fingers. The reminder of how easily he could overpower me was both titillating and terrifying at the same time.

"Fold your legs and straighten your back. Relax."

I closed my eyes and flexed my muscles.

"Your shoulders are too high up. You're looking for relaxation, not constipation."

"I'm trying," I grumbled, curling my lip. I shook my shoulders loose and cracked my knuckles before placing my hands on top of his again.

"Take deep, slow breaths from your diaphragm."

I shut my eyes again and tried not to get distracted from by huskiness of Laz's voice. I wasn't sure what *tawarid mana* required, but I hoped it wasn't much different from meditation. I thought I could do it if I concentrated.

"You're going to have to try to sync to my khwala – my wavelength. Listen to the sound of my voice. Copy my breathing patterns. Pay attention to each beat of my pulse through my palms. Don't say anything. Don't think anything. Let me guide you."

The stitches in his hands were tickling my palms, but I forced that thought to the back of my mind. I held in my breath and exhaled with him. With my eyes closed, I could feel a rhythmic drumming coming from his palms. The more I paid attention to it, the more it seemed as if the noise was getting louder and closer to my ears.

I heard someone else talking.

"Two thousand civilians are believed dead in the Fallgold bloodshed..."

Now it was another voice.

"Private! Get your worthless face off the ground and finish that lap before I rip off your leg and drag you to the finish line!"

A different person now.

"Man down! I repeat, man down! Back off and give him some air. Hang in there, Liam. I'm not going anywhere."

Choppy images and garbled, disembodied voices started invading my mind. They came one after another, but each flashing image lasted for no longer than a second. The worst were scenes of explosions, cities in ruins, and mutilated corpses. My shoulders started shaking, but I didn't notice it until Laz pulled his palms out from under me.

I buckled over, holding my hand against my racing heart.

"Sorry. That's not supposed to happen," said Laz quietly. "I got distracted. Are you okay?"

"I can't believe it. It was like I was in your head," I gasped. My mind was still reeling from the horrifying images. Was that what he lived with every day? I nodded and gave my hands a shake. "Let's try it again."

"Take two."

I placed my palms on his and allowed our breathing to harmonize.

When I closed my eyes, I saw a dusty desert scene in front of me. The difference was that I was no longer looking through my eyes. Judging by the oversized world around me, I was looking out from the eyes of a young Laz who couldn't have been older than five or six.

And I definitely wasn't on Xylox anymore.

* * * *

YOUNG LAZARUS

Along with the sun's dazzling rays beating down on my face, the air felt fresh and exhilarating. Coral-tinted clouds floated across the rolling blue skies. I glanced down at my feet. The small soles of my boots sunk into the gleaming white sand.

I climbed the wavy floors of sand dunes, but as I reached the top, I realized what lay on the other side was far from scenic.

People had erected massive white tents all over an open area, creating a small campsite. A mixture of human and Maztek doctors treated patients both inside the tents and out - the camp was already over capacity. Doctors were even wheeling around small children on appropriately-sized mobile beds. Most of them appeared to be on drugs for their pain. They looked tiny next to their towering IV drips.

I kicked off my boots and swung them next to me as I walked along the crest of the hill. The tiny grains of sand felt fantastic between my bare toes. When I spotted my father and grandfather coming up the dune to our right, we looked for a place to hide and found it beneath a large boulder. I held onto the edge of the rock and carefully peeked around it. I knew this area was out of bounds. Even though they were far away, I would be able to hear their conversation from my hiding place.

Father and Upa put on surgical masks and approached a man in a hazmat suit from behind. The man turned around and lifted his mask over his head. It was Marshall.

"Fahzi," Marshall said. My father had a weary expression on his lined face. He had not slept for a few days. "I think it's far too early in the day to see your ugly mug, Andrei."

"As they say on Earth – blow me, Marshall," Father fired back, grinning. The grim look on his face disappeared as he looked around at the grisly scene. "How's it looking for these patients? Have you made any progress?"

"Our supply of antidote is running dangerously low. I have people working to find the ingredients we need from neighboring ports. Once we get all the components, we can start creating a fresh batch."

"How are we determining who is first in line for the remainder? I assume children are receiving the last of the antidote," Upa piped up, crossing his arms.

My Upa's face was deeply grooved and heavily scarred, and his sleeves could barely contain his muscles. As he spoke, someone approached wheeling a chubby boy with big brown eyes and a handful of tubes running out from his chest. Upa's expression instantly softened as he made a silly face, getting the boy to start giggling. As soon as he turned back to the men, his face was as grim as ever.

"For now," Marshall replied sternly. "The Xylo biological weapons have put these villages in quite a predicament. They've understood for the most part, but tensions are escalating. A few have started to complain, and those in severe pain will begin to make louder demands."

The haunting call of a blow horn ripped through the air.

Surprised by the noise, I fell and landed on my butt with a thud. I jammed my feet into my boots, wanting to flee the scene as quickly as possible. Hurtling down the slope of the dune, I ran straight for Marshall, Father, and Upa.

Soldiers were streaming in from all directions to evacuate the patients and workers, who were starting to panic. Father's eyes bulged, then lit up when he spotted me. He grabbed me by the back of my shirt and held me up by the shoulders.

"Lazarus! I know I told you to stop playing around here. It's going to get dangerous." Father paused and held me in his arms. He turned toward Marshall, who was running towards a tent. "Marshall! You're going in the wrong direction."

"I know there's a patient back there who's senile. We haven't accounted for him. He often hides in the supply closet..."

"Marshall, no! And there he goes. Fuck!" Father thrust me into Upa's arms and started running after Marshall. "We're running out of time. Take Laz and make sure you get him to the shelter!"

My body trembled as Upa opened a circular vault door built into the ground. He pulled back the top and he climbed into the small space, squeezing me along with him. The bunker of last resort was made to house only one man, so adding a young child made it very cramped. I still hadn't uttered a word, but I knew my eyes were wide with fright. Once we settled inside, Upa sealed the door behind us.

"Close your eyes, Laz. There's going to be a little rumble, but it will all be over soon."

The eerie whine of an approaching bomb grew louder than a rumble. Before I could brace myself, the ground above

156

us was hit with a blast that shook the ground. Just as Upa predicted, our chamber vibrated for almost ten seconds.

"It's going to be fine, Laz. Just hold on tightly to me."

Upa climbed the ladder and grunted as he lifted the vault door over his head. He set me on the ground next to him and grabbed my outreached hand. Upa fanned the cloud of dense black smoke permeating the air. Through the fog, we could see that the few remaining tents were ablaze.

Three shadowy figures began limping toward me. As the fog slowly cleared, my knees went weak with relief. Marshall and Father each had an arm of a white-faced patient draped around their necks. They lay him carefully on the ground and promptly fell alongside him. All three lay quietly amidst the wreckage, trying to regain their strength.

* * * *

Laz pulled his hand away. He looked drained and fell back but caught himself with his palms before he hit the ground. My face felt flushed. I rested the back of my head against the edge of the bed. Laz crawled over and sat next to me. He leaned in and gently opened my eyes with his fingers.

"Are you all right in there?"

"I'm okay. Just tired and a little shaken." My eyes drooped shut again as I shook my head sadly. "To think, after all that, Dad died in a horrible shuttle crash."

"Why do you say that?" Laz interjected. He frowned, looking genuinely confused. "Marshall survived the impact."

The hairs on my arms stood up straight, and my blood felt ice-cold.

"Do you know what happened to him?"

"It turned out Synic shot down his shuttle. It's very similar to your situation. Synic took Marshall hostage and interrogated him about Maztek troop deployment."

Laz's words trailed off as he stared at me. I sniffed and wiped off my tears with my fists. He was doing it again – evaluating me with his stony poker face.

"Why are you waiting? What did they do to him? Don't hold back now," I begged. My pitch was rising with every word I spoke. "Don't spare a single detail. What did they do to my father?"

Laz blinked at me.

"Marshall would not give up any information, of course. Synic killed him. They told me it was swift and painless. Your father died a hero."

It was my turn to narrow my eyes and analyze his face. "Are you lying to me?"

Before I could get an answer, the communicator crackled to life.

"General? General, this is Sargeant Major Dallas – do you read me? I repeat, do you read me? Over."

CHAPTER 15

LAZ

I didn't have time to tell Gabriella everything, but when night came, I didn't have control of my dreams. I became a boy once again, reliving my worst nightmares.

"Lazarus! Don't walk so fast."

I rushed back to my father's side at once. Upa broke away from a boar sausage stand filled with meat skewers and joined us. I eagerly took the grilled sausage from my grandfather and started munching on the treat. Upa knew how fond I was of triple-horned boar meat.

"Sorry, Ono."

"Upa and I were finally given time off today, so there's no need to rush. We have the whole day ahead of us."

We wandered down the vibrant streets of Fallgold Plaza. It was Festival Day. Families from all over the planet came to the capital, celebrating the city's rich culture and history. Vendors set up shops along the streets, selling food, desserts, and liquor for shoppers to consume as they enjoyed the festivities. Beautiful women wearing colorful headdresses, make-up, and beads paraded alongside the shoppers. Young men with elaborate masks painted on their faces followed the dancers. The men provided music with their trumpets and drums.

I had a question. "Why do you work so much?" I tossed my empty skewer into the trash can. "Zendaya's parents only work five days a week, and they are always home in time for supper."

My father sighed and exchanged an unreadable look with Upa.

"Zendaya's parents work in a different field. Upa and I have critical jobs with the military." My father knelt down next to me and placed a hand on my back. "Look around you."

The party surrounding us was exciting. I wished I could attend with my family every day. Children waved their hands in the air and stamped their feet gleefully along with the dancers. Loving couples of all ages strolled down the streets hand in hand. I looked back at my father. "It looks like everyone is having fun."

"It is our job to ensure everyone you see here is out of harm's way. Unfortunately, Lazarus, bad things can come from Xylox every day."

"I hope you get all the Xylo, Ono. Maybe then you and Upa can spend more time with me."

"That's a sweet thought, my boy," Upa joined in, chuckling. But if that were the case, your old man and I would be out of a job."

My father grinned as he rose to his feet. "That's right. We'd have to find something else to do. Now, Lazarus, you completed the training course this morning in record time. Why don't you look around and pick out a toy?"

"You mean it, Ono? Anything I want?"

"Aye."

"Thank you."

Before I could say anything else, we heard a sound behind us. We turned toward the spreading gasps in the crowd.

"Up there! What is that? Was there a shuttle show scheduled for today?"

"No, they haven't done that in years..."

Upa and my father grabbed their communicators from their belts at almost the same time and started barking at them. My lip quivered as I stepped back. I had never seen my father behave like this before, and I wondered what it meant. Upa's voice started cracking as he cursed wildly into his communicator. My father cupped his hands around his mouth. He weaved his way through the crowd and rallied everyone around him, getting their attention and telling them to look in the sky.

I turned my head up along with the rest of the crowd. A dozen black and red shuttles were coming toward us. The spacecraft were moving through the clouds and leaving trails of black smoke in the sky.

An announcement blared over the warning system. "This is an evacuation. This is not a drill. I repeat, this is not a drill. Do not panic. Evacuate the area."

They didn't have time to say anything else before the first bomb plunged from the skies and struck the Fallgold bell tower. We watched the majestic gold structure slowly disintegrate into fire and rubble. The ground underneath us cracked from the impact.

That was when the screaming started.

Suddenly everyone who looked like they were in a position of authority or a police officer was grappling with panicked citizens, holding them back to prevent a stampede. Upa and my father were only two more people in the chaos. Upa rattled off instructions to as many of the authorities as he could, but his words fell on deaf ears. My father took a different tactic. He gathered families with young children and lead them to the emergency fallout shelters.

"Lazarus!" My father snatched me up from the ground and thrust me into the arms of a young mother.

"Ono! No, I want to stay with you."

"Please, take my son."

"No, Ono – wait! Let go of me!" The woman managed to drag me for a few feet before I pulled myself away from her grasp. I slid out from her flailing arms and ran as fast as my legs would carry me. The wind whipped against my face. The rising sand kicked up by my feet clouded my vision.

Another explosion ripped through the air.

The next thing I knew, I was landing on the ground. Burning pain shot through my right leg. The intense feeling was the only reason I knew I was still alive. I slowly rolled over to my side, sputtering and coughing uncontrollably. When my eyes finally opened, I screamed.

A bloody, severed arm with a tattoo of my name lay in front of my face.

* * * *

"Laz? Laz, wake up!"

I pressed my fingers to my temples and opened my eyes. The first thing I saw was Gabriella's face in front of me.

"Are you all right? I didn't know if I should let you stay asleep or not. You were tossing and turning all night, and then you started mumbling. I got worried."

"Was I?" My voice was still hoarse. "I'm sorry, I didn't mean to wake you."

"It's fine. I just wanted to make sure there wasn't anything wrong."

Gabriella had already dressed in a silver jumpsuit. She had made the bed, and her belongings were packed into her satchel. She was ready to go. I sat up and rested my back against the foot of the bed. Sleeping on the hard floor for the past few days was starting to affect my posture. I stretched my arms over my head and cracked the knots digging into my spine.

"Quick question for you – what's a naima?"

"It's a word that comes from an old Maztek folk story. Naimas are two kindred souls connected by something in their history, and share a common destiny. In our world, not everyone is lucky enough to find their naima. Many think it's a load of shit. Why do you ask?"

"Huh," said Gabriella thoughtfully. She tilted her head and shrugged. "I could have sworn you said naima the other night."

I froze. I grunted as I heaved myself off the ground, and turned away from her. Not having words to say, I chose to do nothing.

"We should start moving before it gets too late."

* * * *

"General Laz! Glad to see you're alive, sir."

Sergeant Major Dallas ran out of the enclosure. There was a gash across his nose, but it was healing. One of his wings was pinned back with a plaster cast. We pounded our fists on our chests twice and pulled each other in for a hug.

"How is everyone holding up without me?"

"Jarrod and Maxwell didn't make it." Dallas lowered his voice and hung his head. "Other than that, we're surviving."

I paused for a moment, looking at the ground. I didn't want to look weak, but I hated death. Every member of my team was necessary. Jarrod and Maxwell were inseparable numb-skulls, but they would have died for each other.

"This is Gabriella, my bride from Earth." I stepped aside and gestured to Gabriella, who was hovering behind me. "Gabriella, Sargeant Major Dallas."

"Pleased to finally meet you." Dallas nodded at Gabriella, shaking her hand. "I'm sorry it isn't on better terms."

Dallas led us past a perimeter my crew had set up away from Synic's lair. My men were spread out in a campsite. Dirt coated their smeared faces and hands; they had kept themselves busy repairing their equipment. Each stopped working to salute as we walked past.

We approached a large tent built at the back of the enclosure. "Come in here." Dallas held open the flap of the tent opening and waved us inside.

"Whoa..." Behind me, Gabriella sounded like she was in awe.

A couple of my men were fixing up a small Xylo orbiter. The compact craft was painted black with red stripes on the wings. It looked like an attack ship, but right now I thought it would be a great way to get Gabriella off the planet.

"We transported the brides we were able to recover to Maztek yesterday morning," said Dallas. He walked up to the craft and slapped the side of the wing. "This was the only other ship we managed to salvage from the scene.

You and Gabriella should take this one. The rest of us will wait for reinforcements."

"What about the ones you couldn't recover?" Gabriella chimed in softly. "Does that mean they died, or you weren't able to retrieve them?"

"We checked the shuttle's passenger list. Three are missing and presumed dead," Dallas said, sighing regretfully. "We did all we could."

"General! You're going to want to see this."

Dallas and I exchanged troubled glances before we met up with Kraig near the opening of a tent. The rest of the crew dropped what they were doing and assembled around me. Kraig turned up the volume on his computer and held up the thin transparent screen for everyone to see. A pair of somber Maztek reporters appeared on the video feed, sitting on either end of a long table.

"This morning, King Jacquim and Maztek authorities received a video message from Xylo tyrant Synic. A warning to all parents and guardians – the following video contains disturbing imagery, and is not for the faint-hearted."

The feed switched to a video from a different source. The blurry face of a Xylo guard filled the screen. He moved off-camera to focus the shot in the distance before leaving the frame. Synic panned into view with two guards on either side of him.

Each Xylo held a leash in their hands, attached to an electric shock collar fastened around the neck of a disheveled bride. Well, now we knew they were alive, at least. Synic's woman looked like the worst of the three. It was hard to see her face through her thick black curls of hair, but as she raised her head to the camera, I caught a glimpse of a swollen bottom lip and a black eye.

Synic moved his leash slightly. The bride yelped, grabbing onto her collar out of instinct. Synic dramatically raised his hand and pushed the button on a control box. The bride convulsed briefly before crumpling forward, howling in pain. Synic lowered his hand and adjusted the front of his red cloak. He looked directly into the camera without saying anything.

"Cheyenne!"

I glanced to my left. Gabriella was staring at the screen, and it looked like she wanted to run through it and grab the girl.

"As you can see, your Maztek army has failed to complete their mission. We still have three of your precious brides. I require ten million credits for their safe return. I've got better things to do, and my clock is ticking. If we don't receive the funds within twenty-four hours, we will execute one of the Earth women, and we'll keep going until they are all dead. One slip-up and we kill all these whores. Your move, King Jacquim."

The feed went black. Several people started talking at once.

"We need to go get Cheyenne, like right now. How soon can we go?"

"No." I stepped in front of Gabriella and held my feet apart. "The only thing we need to do is to put you on an orbiter and get you out of here."

"What about my friend?"

"We're outnumbered. Protocol calls for us to get the people we have to safety as soon as possible."

"I can't do that. I'm not leaving here without Cheyenne." Gabriella's chin wobbled, and her voice sounded strained. She crossed her arms and grabbed her elbows defiantly. "Please. We're all in this together. None of the brides deserve to be with Synic for another minute. I got lucky, but it could easily have been me in there."

I glared at her for a few moments before growling in defeat. "We know the most information about Synic, but we're going to need some help. Dallas! Round up the crew and see if you can get some reinforcements from home. We're going back."

CHAPTER 16

GABRIELLA

"Morning. Can I come in?"

The cot squeaked as I rolled to my side. A hulking shadow hovered outside the tent opening. I sat up on the bed and smoothed my hair, which was still messy from sleep.

"Go ahead."

Dallas leaned down and slipped in through the tent flaps. He was the only one of Laz's crew that wasn't Maztek. His shoulders were as broad as the hood of a car, and he overshadowed the rest of the soldiers. His injured wing was out of the cast and in its last stages of healing, but he still couldn't fold it to his back.

"How did you sleep last night?" He had the voice of a gentle giant – a deep baritone, but subtly inflected with a hint of calmness.

"It wasn't the cold, hard ground, so I guess I can't complain."

His stark white eyes glowed as he grinned. "I assure you, the sleeping arrangements back home are much better than here." He dug inside his big uniform, which was tailored to his body size. Taking out a sealed brown package, he handed it to me. "The General wanted to make sure you had some breakfast. It's not a big meal, but it should tide you over for now."

"Thank you so much." I ripped open the packet and bit into the flaky yellow pastry. My tongue was pleasantly surprised at the gooey pink filling that tasted like vanilla and caramel custard. "Where is Laz — I mean, the General, anyway?"

"He's outside, planning our entry with the rest of the team. We think we've figured out a different way to enter and will proceed as soon as reinforcements arrive. It shouldn't be long now."

"Thanks for the information." I finished up the rest of my pastry and licked the crumbs off my fingers. "I couldn't get anything out of Laz."

They say females have a knack for giving the cold shoulder, but I've learned that males are equally proficient. Laz wasn't exactly ignoring me, but he had gone back to his simple, one-word replies. I knew he didn't want me to be on Xylox still, but I felt like I didn't have a choice.

I wouldn't have been able to live myself if I abandoned Cheyenne. Even if I couldn't be part of the rescue operation, I felt better knowing I was on the planet for her. I wondered if I would die here in a useless sacrifice. It would be an ironic death. Dad didn't have to die, but he was too noble to protect himself. If the extraction failed, I might suffer a similar fate.

Dallas broke the silence and nodded his head. "Give the General some time. He'll come around sooner or later. If it counts for anything, I understand why you decided to stay here. He does too. It may not have been a wise decision, but it was honorable."

"I don't even know her that well. We met on the flight over here."

"Many honorable actions are founded on stupidity."

"Thanks, I think."

Before Dallas could reply, a Maztek I hadn't seen before appeared by the tent entrance. The bright-faced and clean-shaven stranger wore combat gear, but unlike what I had seen before, gold and silver trimmings embellished his. The weapons in his belt were gilded and seemed more elaborate than the others I had seen, but they looked well-used.

Dallas pounded his fist against his chest and stomped his feet before saluting the stranger.

"King Jacquim."

I had just woken up. I wanted to look my best for royalty, but I knew my hair was a mess, and my face was probably puffy. Panicking, I jumped off the bed and dropped to my knees, sprawling over in a deep bow.

"You must be Gabriella. You don't have to do that. Please, stand up."

I stumbled as the king held out his arm and helped me to my feet. As King Jacquim chuckled, his perfect white-blond waves bounced around his strong, dimpled chin. I chewed on my lip and started rambling.

"Sorry, I've never actually met royalty before, Your Highness. Do I even call you 'Your Highness'? Or would you prefer 'Your Excellency'?"

"That's all nonsense," said the King, flicking his wrist. The King's amber eyes shone as he flashed me perfect rows of pearly white teeth. "You do not come from Maztek, so there should be no reason for you to refer to me as anything but Jacquim. If you must, King is more than adequate."

"As you wish, Your – uh – King Jacquim."

The king stepped aside from the opening as Laz popped into the tent as well. It was starting to get crowded in here. Laz's eyes widened briefly at the unexpected sight of the king, but he quickly regained himself and greeted him.

"King Jacquim. I wasn't aware you were joining us on this mission. Is it wise to risk the King's life in this manner?"

"I would not miss it for the world. We're not going to give in on any of Synic's demands while I'm still alive. This war has gone on for too long. With your help, it may end today."

"For now, there's food and drink waiting for you all in Delta-4B. We could all use the nourishment."

"Dallas, take Gabriella with you," said Laz, retreating out of the tent. "Excuse me. I have other business to attend to."

* * * *

No one would ever accuse the Maztek military of being undisciplined. At 8:30 p.m. on the dot, the crew set out. Maztek soldiers filed into five separate military shuttles. Once they bolted the doors, the state-of-the-art spacecraft silently launched from the ground and zipped off into the night. Laz and I were left behind to follow suit in the two-seater Xylo shuttle his men had salvaged.

I slung my satchel over my shoulder and approached Laz from behind. The hatch on the side of the shuttle was open. He squatted next to the doorway, flipping switches and opening control boxes to make sure everything was working.

"Laz."

He glanced over his shoulder at me before returning to his last minute tasks.

"You ready?"

"I think so." I pulled my satchel in front of me and drew out a container filled with military rations I had packed for him. "You never showed up to the party. It's going to be a big night. Accomplishing anything on an empty stomach is hard. I know, I've been there."

"You didn't have to do that." Laz turned back to face me. He raised one eyebrow as he accepted the container. "But thank you. I'll eat this later."

"It's not a problem. I'm your wife now." I said lightly. "You've been watching out for me for so long that I better start doing the same for you. Is there anything I can do to help?"

"I don't think so. I'm just wrapping up here." Laz reached for something on the wall and hopped out of the shuttle, holding a weapon. He tossed it to me.

"This is for you."

I yelped and dove for the gun. The brassy rose-gold pistol was heavier than I expected.

"Don't worry. The safety is engaged. You're going to have to wait in one of the shuttles until we return, so I'm giving you a lightweight pistol for protection. It's not the most powerful weapon we have in stock, but it should be enough to protect you without my worrying that you'll accidentally kill yourself. I'm going to leave it with you in case anything happens. Have you ever fired a gun?"

I shook my head, feeling a chill of intimidation.

"I went to a shooting range once after one of my fights with Jake to blow off some steam, but I was horrible at it. I'm not great at the aiming thing. I wouldn't trust me with a water gun."

Laz cracked his first smile of the day. "Fortunately for you, there's a stabilizing feature built into this model. Come with me."

Laz walked behind the shuttle and set up five empty cans. He stood a good distance way from the targets and motioned me to come closer. I walked up to him, pointing the gun at the ground, holding it with both hands. My rattling heart pounded harder against my chest when Laz positioned himself behind me. Did he have to stand this close to me? I could feel the bristles of his beard lightly tickling the nape of my neck.

"Relax. I'll walk you through it."

"I'm as relaxed as I can get with this death machine."

"Don't be dramatic. Raise your weapon with one hand and keep it steady with the other."

I did as he told me but my arms were starting to hurt from the weight of the pistol.

"I'm going to need to place my hands on yours to show you what to do. Is that okay?"

I nodded, swallowing to soothe my dry throat. My hands disappeared from view as Laz wrapped his rough, strong fingers over mine. I liked the way his palms felt against my flesh. It was a testament to all the manual labor he had performed over the years.

"Turn off the safety feature on the right side of the weapon, and loosely put one of your fingers on the trigger."

My palms were getting sweatier by the second. It was a miracle the pistol hadn't flown out of my fingers. Laz raised my stretched arms to eye-level and aligned the can to the gun sight. I squeezed one eye shut and peered through the sight posts. With his finger guiding mine, he gently pulled back the trigger.

A bolt of blue laser fire blasted out the mouth of the pistol, knocking down the can in the middle.

"Go ahead. Give it a try yourself." He removed his hands, leaving me alone.

I started shaking, but I felt the pistol stabilizing itself in my grip. I pulled back on the trigger five times in succession. Blue bolts flew out the weapon, striking two of the four remaining cans. Satisfied, I turned the safety on again and whirled around giddily to face Laz.

"I suppose that will have to do." He jerked his head towards the shuttle. "We should go. The crew is waiting for us."

* * * *

I leaned my elbows against the armrests of the shuttle seat and nestled my head in my hands. To make up for the time lost at the impromptu shooting practice, Laz had flown the shuttle over to Synic's base faster than I had ever gone before. I unfastened my seatbelt and clamped a hand over my mouth.

"Did we have to go so fast?"

"If you need to throw up, there's an empty bucket somewhere in the back," said Laz without looking up at me. He was busy performing a double-check of the equipment in his satchel and on his person.

"I think I'll be fine, as long as I never fly again."

"We're leaving now. Keep the door locked. If all goes well, we'll be back in less than an hour."

"I will," I promised. I wasn't sure what to do. Should I kiss him goodbye? Hug him? Fuck him because he might die? I wet my lips as I reached over, deciding to touch him tentatively on the shoulder. "Laz? Be careful."

Laz stared at my hand. He blinked at me and nodded, ducking out the shuttle door. I secured all the locks and dimmed the lights. Peering out the window of the shuttle, I watched the Maztek lower themselves down the edge of the cliff. The plan was to take Synic by surprise from above. One by one, the men faded into the darkness of the abyss.

I trotted to the pilot seat and sat in front of the dark cockpit controls. I started to entertain myself with the irresistibly bright buttons and limited shuttle features. Unsurprisingly, pretending to be a deep-space explorer lost its luster in minutes. However, in the midst of my bored random poking, I discovered a small game hidden in the cockpit screen.

The 8-bit graphic adventure was mindless but entertaining. It was probably installed to provide Xylo pilots with something to do while they waited for their away teams to return. Now it was doing the same thing for me.

I don't know how long I had been playing the game before I heard the voices. I sat up immediately and peered out the tinted windows. Two Xylo soldiers were poking around the Maztek shuttles. My breath caught in my throat. As they approached the first ship, they started firing at the doors. Steel bullets rang loudly in the quiet of the night, ricocheting off the thick metal.

The soldiers cried out and grumbled, but as soon as they spotted my Xylo shuttle, they stopped talking and moved toward it.

"Shit."

I grabbed the pistol from the seat next to me and slid down to the ground, squeezing myself into a space under the cockpit controls. I heard their footsteps growing louder as they approached the shuttle doors. They didn't need to fire bullets at this ship; they knew how to enter a spacecraft of their design. I hear a loud beep as the locks disengaged. The doors whirred open.

My eyes grew wide at the two pairs of boots leaving clouds of black dust as they paced around the cockpit. Would they see me? They looked around the ship but thankfully avoided my hiding spot.

The soldiers angrily muttered in defeat as they turned away to leave the shuttle. That was when I felt it - a fluttery tickle rising in my nostrils that I couldn't ignore.

When the loud sneeze came out of my mouth, they both looked at me, raising their weapons.

CHAPTER 17

LAZ

I had forgotten how much easier combat was when people worked together. In the corridor before me, a dozen Xylo soldiers lay on the dirty floor. I stepped carefully over the one in my path, avoiding the puddle of blood coming from the wounds on his throat. My hand signaled to my squad, silently directing them to conceal the bodies in case we needed to make a rapid retreat.

If everything went to plan, we would be in and out of this place in an hour. We had split into four teams for this part of the operation, evenly dividing our forces into units led by myself, Dallas, Kraig, and King Jacquim. The different groups of troops were independently responsible for eliminating the soldiers on the outskirts of Synic's fortress. After we had taken care of the enemy forces, we were supposed to reunite and infiltrate the core of the lair together.

In theory, we would escort the hostages to safety after surrounding Synic and his remaining soldiers. The best possible scenario involved Synic's surrender. None of us wanted to get into a firefight with civilians at risk. After his arrest, he would be arraigned, tried, and sentenced.

In theory.

But one thing I knew about Synic was that bloodshed was inevitable.

Synic's bizarre avian obsession was on prominent display through the ghastly aesthetics of his headquarters. He chose to show headdresses made from exotic bird feathers on the ragged walls. A collection of moldy and deformed stuffed vultures with multiple heads and appendages hung from the leaking ceilings. Strangely there were no live birds, rodents, or even insects.

Everything in the underground chambers had the scent of death, even the technology. The rooms contained a lot of equipment, but what was here seemed to be on its last legs. Synic's technicians had left carts with missing wheels and disemboweled shuttle parts to rust in random corners of the building. It looked as if Synic had once enjoyed top-of-the-line toys, but he had neglected them over the past few decades.

My communicator vibrated, playing an incoming message from Dallas. "General – we are in position and are now on standby."

"Copy that." I held the communicator close to my mouth and spoke quietly into the microphone. "Stand down and wait for my call."

A few of my men moved at my command, slinking off to search for any other ways to get more information about Synic's defenses. I instructed the rest of my men to fall back in the tunnel and enlisted the help of Wyla as my backup. The young nineteen-year-old soldier was small but made up for what she lacked in size in speed, agility, and a supernatural ability to focus. She was also one of the best shots I had ever seen and competent in hand-to-hand combat.

Wyla and I headed west down the tunnel, counting the air ducts until we found one that lead to Synic's security control room. I crouched down and boosted her off the ground. She pulled out a drill and started unscrewing the bolts. Squeezing her fingers through the grills, she wrenched off the vent opening and shined a light into the duct tunnel. Wyla shook off the dust from her bright pink hair.

"It smells worse than the men's bunkers in the summertime, but it's clear."

"Good. You've shared a room with Kraig for two consecutive summers. I'm sure the odor won't be a problem for you."

Wyla rolled her eyes. She shimmied up the duct and extended her arm to me, helping pull me to her level. I took the light from her and moved to take the point. We moved down the tube, looking through the vents underneath us and using the rooms as markers.

I stopped when I heard a noise behind me. Wyla was loudly clicking her tongue against the roof of her mouth. Had I missed something? She moved her chin down, motioning to the vent between us. I was thankful there was a lot of background noise. The hissing and clanking from the aged pipelines behind the walls masked the sounds of the ducts groaning from our weight. I put my head close to the grill to get a better view.

The security control room was directly underneath us. The walls contained several flat screen monitors featuring live camera feeds from all over the lair. We had wondered why our entry had been relatively effortless, and how we could gain access to the compound without triggering any alarms. Now I knew why.

The soldiers manning security were neglecting their duties. Some of Synic's guards had their monitors set to games or configured to display underground fight club matches. The ones who weren't near computers were wasting time in different ways. Some were playing with a homemade brown ball made from metal scraps. Others read magazines while chugging back bottles of liquor.

"Check out the asshole on the far right," Wyla whispered. She wrinkled her button nose and made a disgusted face. "He's either the most stupid or most admirable Xylo on the planet. I can't imagine anyone pursuing such bold extracurricular activities on company time."

Curious, I steered my eyes to the soldier Wyla indicated and laughed. His desktop featured a full-screen slide show of overweight Xylo women posing in schoolgirl outfits. However, with every passing photograph, it became more difficult for me to determine if the subjects were actually all women. The bony guard rocked back and forth in his chair, noisily sucking on his teeth and rubbing the crotch of his pants like he was trying to put out a fire.

"It's time to put an end to this party." I removed my laser pistol from my holster and turned off the safety. Wyla twisted a silencer around her drill, unscrewing the bolts from the vent. As she removed the last bolt, the guard with a penchant for male and female Xylo jerked back in his seat. He looked around him wildly until his eyes latched onto the wobbling grill of the vent duct overhead.

The Xylo screamed a warning. The other guards rose out of their seats at once, scrambling for their weapons. They weren't fast enough. Wyla and I opened fire, striking all the soldiers at the control station before anyone could ring an alarm. The guard on the far right keeled over and slid down his seat, perishing with a tent in his trousers.

"Watch out!"

Wyla and I rolled away from the vent opening as the remaining Xylo retaliated with weapons fire. We pulled ourselves out of the way just in time - one of the soldiers hurled a metal ball in our direction. A thunderous explosion echoed through the vent and a noticeable dent from the collision appeared only a few centimeters from Wyla's nose.

I retreated, narrowly missing the solid line of fire. A trail of bullet holes stopped shortly between my legs. When I looked up, I saw the shells embedded in the ceiling were still smoking. There was a pause of silence. I assumed they were reloading. We moved back to the opening for our chance to retaliate.

Wyla pointed her weapon away from the soldiers. She peered into the mirror, studying the positions of the remaining Xylo. Tapping two fingers against her raised fist, she told me two guards were on my side, and one on hers. I nodded in reply, showing her a countdown with my fingers.

I squeezed one eye shut and gazed intently into my scope. Aiming it at a soldier taking cover behind a file cabinet, I breathed out slowly and pulled on the trigger. It was a straight shot between the eyes, splitting open the back of his head. He lurched backward and smeared the walls with his blood as he slunk to the ground. Wyla had already eliminated her two soldiers in half the time it had taken me.

"I know there's one more," Wyla muttered, holding her laser pistol to her chest. She squinted into the vent. "Come out and play, you elusive piece of shit."

My ears perked up at a faint ticking sound in the room. "Is that a bomb? With a timer? How primitive."

A pale fist reached out from behind a couch, tossing a palm-sized red ball in our direction. I grabbed Wyla and yanked her to my side of the vent. The explosive flew up and landed next to my feet. As the lights on the circular disc began blinking erratically, I reacted without thinking. I snatched up the bomb and threw it back where it came from, behind the couch.

"Let's move out of here!" I shoved Wyla forward and started crawling. Wyla and I made it about twenty feet before the bomb detonated. A tumultuous bang from our rear made the ventilation tunnels begin to sway. The odor of burnt rubber and filled the air. We kept our eyes straight ahead, crawling further away until the tube stabilized.

"That was close," said Wyla, wheezing. "Should we proceed to the core chambers, General?"

I opened my mouth to give her the okay, but I swiftly fell silent at the activity below us. I heard a familiar voice that sent chills down my spine.

"I told you bastards to get your fucking hands off me!"

I waved at Wyla and made eye contact with her, gesturing with my gun. She nodded, silently inching over to work on the next vent cover. I leaned toward the hole in front of me, fighting against panic and attempting to observe the scene unfolding in the corridor.

Two Xylo guards had their arms hooked under Gabriella, dragging her behind them. She kicked out her legs repeatedly in futile desperation, trying to get a grip on the floor with the heels of her feet. I inhaled sharply, feeling my muscles start to flex when I saw the red marks on Gabriella's neck. Her head turned from one side to another as she looked for any way to escape.

"I said, let me go, you alien motherfuckers!"

"That's enough out of you." The guard on Gabriella's right swung his fist and clipped her in the mouth. I growled, looking over at Wyla, who was easing out the final bolt from the cover. Wyla nodded at me, set a line against the edge and jumped out of the vent, attacking the soldiers from above. She didn't even unclip the rope from her belt before she kicked a soldier in the jaw, knocking him off his feet.

I jumped down from the ceiling, prepared to fight the remaining Xylo. But as I turned to Gabriella with my body tensed to lunge at the other guard, I discovered that

Gabriella had taken care of herself. She took advantage of Wyla's distraction and bit down on the guard's hand. He cried out in pain, releasing his prisoner and starting to look at his arm.

The distraction helped me approach from behind. I aimed my laser at the back of his head and executed him. Gabriella started shaking when she saw me.

"Take it easy." I caught Gabriella as she teetered backward, helping her regain composure and keeping her upright. "Are you all right?"

"I think so. I'm okay." She massaged her jaw with a groan. "I don't know what happened. I should have told you when I saw those guys snooping around the shuttle, but I panicked and tried to run. My jaw hurts."

A loud crack came from behind me. Wyla rose from the ground. She dusted her hands nonchalantly and stepped away from the limp-necked guard.

"Don't worry, General. I'll take care of her."

"You're coming with us. Stay close to Wyla, and keep your eyes peeled." Gabriella nodded. "Whatever you do, try to stay out of sight and avoid any confrontation."

I slid against the wall with the barrel of my laser pointed out. When I was sure there were no other soldiers around, I motioned them over. Even though Gabriella was taller than Wyla by a few inches, Wyla took control and guided Gabriella along the corridor behind me.

We crept down the empty passage towards the core chambers, only stopping when we heard distant chatter. I signaled for them to halt and leaned against the wall for a better view. Three soldiers paced around an industrial sliding door which served as one of the entrances to the chambers. Dirty windows provided a murky glimpse into the room holding the hostages.

I motioned to Wyla, assigning her to the opposite wall. We fired at the three guards. The guards slumped to the floor and expired instantly; they never knew what hit them. Wyla and I tiptoed to the doors and peeked through the smudged windows.

Synic's crew was still cleaning up the aftermath of our previous rescue mission. Soldiers worked on machinery and transported raw materials to all levels of the chamber. On the floor, a team of technicians was restoring Synic's weapons and equipment.

The hostages drew attention from my eyes. They were difficult for me to miss, somehow remaining apart from all the distractions in the background. The brides lay in cages suspended from a rail on the second story. Below them, the construction crews had worked to excavate a hole, exposing a pit of sulfurous lava flowing underground.

The beautiful bride on the leftmost cage wept as she stared at the hissing pit below her. The human in the center relentlessly paced inside her cage as she twisted the ends of her bright copper hair. Gabriella's friend, Cheyenne, occupied the final cell. She slouched against the back of the cage, resting her head on her shoulder at an awkward angle. I saw a faint hint of dried blood under her nostrils.

I spotted Synic standing on a platform next to the lava pit, talking with a group of Xylo officials. I slowly looked over the scene again, taking note of all the potential targets. One of the soldiers on the ground had a card that I thought would open the door. Wyla led Gabriella to cover as I activated my communicator.

"Is everyone in position? Let's go."

The heavy metal doors groaned and started to open after I held the ID card next to the scanner. My men burst in from all directions, starting the raid.

The scene changed in an instant. On all levels, Maztek soldiers appeared, shoving the Xylo thugs against the wall. King Jacquim, Dallas, and Kraig moved toward Synic and the officials, raising their weapons and surrounding them. Two brides dropped to their knees and placed their arms over their heads; Cheyenne did not move. Synic raised his hands in surrender and urged his companions to do the same. The perplexed officials reluctantly followed suit.

King Jacquim broke away from the rest of our military. With his gold laser pistol glittering underneath the lights, the king marched toward Synic, only stopping when he reached the platform. He had acquired a pair of restraints somewhere.

"Synic, I am afraid it is the end of the road for you. Hand over your hostages and surrender to us. Let me tell you how this is going to work. As long as you and your men come peacefully with us, there will be no problems. We have you surrounded. It would be foolish to try anything."

It was impossible to decipher what was going on behind Synic's expressionless mask. Synic hung his head in defeat, taking a step forward.

"I don't think so." Without warning, Synic spun around and made a motion with his wrist, pulling a Maztek laser pistol into his hand. Apparent drawing a weapon was the signal for the Xylo resistance force to start fighting back. Synic opened fire around him, and a hail of suppressing blasts came from overhead. They hit two of my men on the second level. I saw their bodies topple over a railing, and I knew they were dead before they even hit the ground. Pandemonium exploded in the chamber, with Xylo and Maztek forces clashing on every level.

Dallas was still injured but extended his wings, grunting as he forced himself into flight. He soared directly to the hostages. Veins popped from his arms as he lowered the cages one at a time to the ground. Two of my men snipped off the locks on the first two cages, picked up the occupants, and headed for the escape hatch.

Overhead, Dallas pulled Cheyenne out from her cage himself. He scooped her into his arms as her thick black hair swept across the floor. As she slowly regained consciousness, Dallas spread his good wing and folded it over her. He made his way to the escape hatch after the other brides, firing at the guards in his path.

A Xylo soldier charged at me, swinging with an iron morning star over his head. But when I shot him in the chest, he fell to the ground. I pulled the spiked mace out of the soldier's grip and flung it in Synic's direction.

The morning star wasn't designed as a throwing weapon. Instead of smashing into Synic's face, it smashed into his cloak, tangling its spikes into the hem. The unexpected weight pulled Synic to his knees. I jumped at the chance to attack and pounced on top of him. I pinned Synic's arms against his body with my legs, immobilizing him as I reached for a set of handcuffs.

This close, I realized there was something odd about Synic. He was more slender than I would have expected. Did he wear a cloak for dramatic effect, or was there a reason he concealed his body? With a frown, I reached for his mask, sliding it off his face and letting it slide into the lava below.

The tyrant in front of me had a smooth face, and sleek, straight black hair. Synic didn't need the mask for health reasons after all. Synic needed the mask to conceal the fact that she was a woman.

I didn't think she was much older than myself. She was definitely from Xylox, but the years spent behind a mask had protected her from the physical deformities common to a native. Her gray-tinged skin revealed red and pink veins in her body. She had wide pupils, so large that they almost drowned out the whites of her eyes. Her eyes defiantly stared at me.

Her gender was irrelevant. Woman or not, this person and her family were responsible for all the Maztek lives needlessly lost and irreparably damaged from the Xylox wars. On a personal level, thoughts of Gabriella, Marshall, Upa, and father sprang to my mind. Thousands of families broken forever.

Synic cried out in anger. "Unhand me, you blood traitor!" Without the voice distortion behind the mask, her voice sounded eerily childlike.

I held Synic's wrists together with one hand, ready to apply the handcuffs, when Gabriella's screams rang out behind me.

"Laz! Look out!"

A shadow loomed behind me. I had to release Synic and roll off her. On my back, I could see what the threat was: a bulky Xylo soldier, unarmed but ready to kill with his hands. I pulled out my pistol and shot him twice in the chest. He fell backward and crashed to the ground, twitching.

"Oh my God!" Gabriella cried out behind me. "Laz, are you okay?"

I leaped to my feet as I caught sight of two soldiers approaching Gabriella. I needed to protect her more than I needed to feed my lust for revenge. I fired at the new threat and reached for her arm, pulled her in tightly.

"What are you doing here? Where's Wyla?"

"I don't know."

The sound of a door closing made us both turn our heads. We saw part of a torn red cloak slip through an escape hatch.

CHAPTER 18

GABRIELLA

No one felt the need to explain everything to the Earth girl, but from the pieces of eavesdropped conversation I overheard, the Xylo soldiers who kidnapped me had also damaged the communication systems and engines of the Maztek shuttles. They said other things too, but it was all too technical for me. All I knew for sure was that the shuttles were temporarily unfit for travel. A repair crew was constantly working to service the spaceships and get them running as soon as possible. At a minimum, it looked like we were stuck on Xylox until dawn.

We had joined three tents together, making a relatively large space under the linked roofs. Inside the tents, the air had the taste of hesitant excitement. Synic had escaped, but the Xylo high command were now Maztek prisoners, ready to go to trial. The Maztek considered the battle an interim victory. After they delivered the human brides to Maztek, they planned to come back and permanently deal with the Synic problem.

I poured a small helping of stew into a bowl. The rich red stew was nice and thick, floating with meat chunks, potatoes, and fragrant spices. I had hit my physical limit over the past few days trying to evade the Xylo, and I felt like I could eat everything here by myself.

The cooking crew had pushed folding tables together and laid out platters of barbecued meat, vibrant salads, sweet cakes, and drinks on them. A few of the army men had brought out some musical instruments, providing live tunes for the get-together. King Jacquim wasn't afraid to dance by himself. He flipped over an empty fuel barrel, drumming along to the beat.

Two human brides sat together in a corner of the tent, talking among themselves behind brimming plates of food. I smelled the aroma of freshly washed hair behind me.

"Hey, you."

An arm swooped in and squeezed me from behind. I set my bowl down on the side of the table and turned around. Cheyenne stood before me, beaming. Her right arm was in a sling, and she had changed into a loose long-sleeved nightgown. The swelling on her eye and busted lip had gone down considerably, but the bruising on her face was still prominent. My eyes welled up as I threw my arms around her, hugging her tightly.

"I can't believe you made it. We owe everything to the Maztek military." I broke away from her, pulling out strands of her hair from my mouth.

"Dallas said you wouldn't leave without being part of the team to get me." Her voice was still raspy from all her screaming. I felt a sharp prick in my chest. I hadn't known Cheyenne for a long time, but she was my best friend out in space. "I don't know how to thank you. I don't think I could have held on for much longer if the Mazteks hadn't shown up when they did. I was ready to jump."

"Are you kidding me? I would have done it again if I had to. We're about to start a new life on a new planet. I need

194

a friend to hang with, go for an ice cream social with, compare alien cock sizes, whatever."

"Ice cream socials, huh? That does sound like a peachy good time." Cheyenne's eyes twinkled. She sighed, and her smile vanished. "The fact of the matter is, I'm not sure how long I'm going to stay on Maztek."

"What do you mean?"

"It turns out my husband thought I was one of the brides who died in the crash." Cheyenne shrugged, but her voice was thick with disappointment. "He went ahead and got himself a new bride already. We've only been away from Earth for less than a week. I'm not bitter, but my citizenship converted back to a visitor's visa. King Jacquim told me he could extend it a little longer. Hopefully, a royal edict will help grease the wheels. I hear it's a tedious process."

As my gaze floated over Cheyenne's shoulders, a smile returned to my face. "I wouldn't be so sure about that."

Cheyenne furrowed her brows and turned around, following my line of sight. Sargeant Major Dallas sat across the room with a handful of his comrades. The soldiers tipped back mugs of ale as they played an obscure game with several pieces of four-sided Maztek dice.

"Dallas?"

"He's looked over here four times since we've started talking." I ran my tongue over my lips. "Trust me. I've been here for half an hour, and he didn't take his eyes off the game until you came around."

"I should go over there and thank him, shouldn't I? I mean, he did get me out of that horrible place," Cheyenne said thoughtfully, nibbling on her thumbnail. She nodded, answering her question. "Yeah, I should. I guess I'll see you a little later then."

"Make sure you do everything you possibly can to thank him."

Cheyenne tentatively started moving toward the handsome Zagwog soldier. I picked up my bowl and reached for a spoon from the utensil station, leaning against the table. Mindlessly stirring but not eating any of the perfectly good soup, my eyes wandered around the tent.

My face froze when I spotted Wyla and Laz. Quietly, I inched toward the tent pillar closest to me. I partially concealed myself behind the pillar as I shoveled a spoonful of stew into my mouth.

Wyla couldn't relax. She stood at attention, with her arms behind her and her feet apart. Her bouncing pink hair was the only thing that moved when she spoke. The more I looked at her oddly-colored hair, the more it reminded me of cotton candy. It was strange – as I stayed away from Earth longer, unusual sights began to trigger memories of the most insignificant things from back home. I didn't even like the sticky pink treat but knowing that I no longer had the option to decline the candy made me want it all the more.

Laz's brooding face didn't change expression as he stormed out of the tent.

"I'm sorry I let her get away from me, General," Wyla called out after him. "You have my word it will not happen again."

I left my bowl on the table and hurried towards Wyla.

"I hope I didn't get you into too much trouble."

She glanced up at me, her violet eyes flashing angrily. "Not now, Gabriella."

Wyla deliberately moved away from me and stalked off to the drink station. Sighing, I hung my head. Maybe I would have better luck with Laz. Not wanting to burst any bubbles with a bad attitude, I navigated past the celebrating army men with a smile plastered on my face. After halfheartedly obliging the King with a round of a Maztek folk dance that I didn't know, I finally made it out of the tent.

The music and gaiety faded into the night as I moved across the site. I rubbed my arms, shivering in the cold. Laz's quarters were in an exclusive area. King Jacquim, Laz, and the brides were the only ones with private tents. The rest of the crew were sharing rooms together. They were rotating shift duties for shuttle repairs and guarding the campsite.

I lingered for a while in front of the tent. When I finally gathered my courage, I pulled back one side of the opening and peered inside.

"Can I come in?"

"If you must." Laz grunted.

I slipped quickly into the tent but promptly froze after I entered. Laz was naked from the waist up, bench-pressing a barbell with four heavy weights on both sides. Every hollow of his abs and every jutting vein on his sweaty tanned muscles gleamed with sweat. I turned away, not wanting to seem creepy but wanting to look back at the same time.

"I'm sorry. I can return later if you're busy."

Laz put down the barbell and sat up, reaching for a towel next to him.

"Do you need something?"

I folded my hands. "I saw you with Wyla earlier. I thought you should take it easy on her. It wasn't her fault. The Xylo soldiers came out of nowhere, and she was fighting them off. I saw the other soldier coming up on you. I reacted without thinking."

"You should have stayed where you were like I ordered you to." Laz rubbed a towel over his face and chest. "I was close to getting that fucker, but she still got away."

"I don't know what to say," I muttered. I took a deep breath. "I'm not sure how many more times I can apologize to you before the universe explodes. You guys saved all the human brides. Doesn't that count for something, even if Synic is still roaming free?" I held my breath. I didn't know if it counted for anything in Laz's book.

"You're right." Laz shifted in his seat and leaned forward. The bench creaked under his weight. "I'm sorry. It's not your fault. It's not Wyla's fault. It's not even Synic's fault. I have no one to blame but myself. The General of one of the most elite forces in the galaxy choked under pressure.

"Move over." I prodded him with my finger until he made space for me, then I sat next to him on the bench, crossing my legs. "Are you refusing to join us in the other tent so you can have a pity party for yourself in here? Shit happens that we don't have any control over. Many things could have made a person freeze. Realizing Synic was a woman after thinking she was a man your entire life and reacting to the daughter of the asshole who killed your family were both terrible things. You shouldn't blame yourself for the one time out of a hundred you make a mistake. Instead, you should celebrate the times you succeed."

Laz exhaled from the corner of his mouth, stroking his beard. "It could be because I'm exhausted, but I think you're starting to make a lot of sense."

"Funny," I snorted, raising my hand to punch him lightly on the arm. Laz caught my fist and squeezed it. I laughed, biting my lip. "Damn you and your cat-like reflexes."

I blushed as I gazed into the green ocean in his eyes. If I didn't know any better, I could have sworn he fully intended to look at me with a smoldering expression that set my body on fire. As he let go of my hand, I let my palm fall on his knee. He didn't move it away.

I tilted my head and leaned closer to him, licking my lips seductively. Laz said nothing, but I could see he was breathing faster. Once I was close enough to feel the soft hairs of his beard tickle my chin, I pressed my lips against his, kissing him deeply.

As soon as our lips connected, I felt something. It was like all our pent-up sexual energy came crashing through a dam.

Laz spun me around on the bench, prying open my legs, and pulling me close to him. He licked my bottom lip and sucked it hungrily. My tongue desperately invaded his mouth as I ran my hands over every delectable inch of his toned chest. I whimpered, feeling a trickle of my juices beginning to moisten my panty lining.

I pulled my mouth away from his, moving behind his ear. I ran my tongue across the cartilage of his ear and down his earlobe, following the natural progression to his neck and chest. I could taste the faint trace of brine from his hot, sweaty workout on my tongue. The insides of my thighs quivered eagerly. I was ready for more. The taste and touch of the raw masculine form in front of me was quickly becoming too much to handle.

"Hold on," I purred in his ear. "Let me make it easier for you."

I crawled away from him and hopped off the bench. Laz stared intently, his eyes boring into me as he watched every move I made. I pulled the zipper of my jumpsuit all the way down to my belly button. I seductively wiggled my shoulders, sliding out of the jumpsuit, which fell to my ankles. I felt the rush of cold air brush against my bare flesh. Covering my breasts with my arm, I sat daintily on the opposite end of the bench, cradling the seat between my legs.

With a wink, I lowered my arm to my side, exposing my chest to the cold air and Laz. My breasts spilled out clumsily. The nipples were erect and pointed directly at him. I eased my legs apart, nudging my hips forward. The wetness leaking out of my quivering pussy lips left a shiny damp mark on the bench.

My rasping moans cut through the air as I taunted him. I pushed two of my fingers through my lips and swirled them around my mouth to lubricate them. Then I circled my wet fingertips around my nipples before moving between my legs. I played with the button of my clit before rubbing up and down my slippery folds.

"I'm nice and wet."

There was no going back now. I knew my body possessed the power to make him do anything. I had him in the palm of my hand. This knowledge filled me with an electrifying force, energizing every move.

Laz clenched his jaw, stroking the bulge in his pants.

"I want you to ravage me and make me cum until I can't see." My sweet smile disappeared as I changed my tone. "That is a fucking order."

"Yes, Ma'am." Laz smiled, the tip of his long tongue poking out the side of his mouth. "I thought you'd never ask."

Laz stripped off his pants and flung them aside. I smacked my lips, my knees trembling at his unexpected size. I wondered if all Maztek were blessed with enormous cocks, or if he was exceptionally well-endowed.

He sat back down on the bench and leaned against the wall, stretching out his legs in front of him. Grabbing me again by my ankles, he reeled me in, positioning me over his lap. I wrapped my legs firmly around his waist. He squeezed my breasts together, licking a line down the gap in my cleavage. I sucked on my lip, throwing my head back as I felt his hot lips close around my left nipple. My hands clung to the back of his shoulders for balance. As he caressed my other breast, he pinched my tender nipple with his teeth.

Feeling an extra flush of juices escaping my sex, I cried out. I brushed the pulsing tip of his cock against my drenched lips to wet it, marveling and touching his veined muscle with my hands. Laz's eyes burned into mine as he eased my hands off his erection and moved them gently to my side. He grabbed his cock with his hands, leering at me. With a smoldering smile, he thrust his cock between the lips of my pussy. I felt my core stretch around him.

"Oh my God, Laz."

My toes curled so forcefully that they were starting to get sore. I dug my nails into his back, losing control of my writhing body. I could feel the tip of his cock grinding against my tingling cervix. The feeling of my pussy squeezing around his thick cock made me want to bounce up and down on it. My sex was wetter than it had ever been before, and it begged for more of Laz's touch, moving with a mind of its own.

Laz gripped the hair on the back of my head. He pulled me in, kissing me passionately. I tasted every part of his mouth, kissing him back sloppily as I rode him harder and harder. His hand slithered between our grinding bodies. As I felt his fingers kneading my clit, I cried out in surprise.

"Please, please don't stop..."

I could feel him smiling as our ravenous lips found each other once more. He went one step further. As he continued to stroke my clit, he stuck out a finger, eased it into my folds, and further stretched out my pussy. I squeezed my eyes shut, letting out a primal groan. For the first time, without having my fingers or vibrator, I could feel the numbing sweetness of climax approaching.

"I'm almost there..."

My juices cascaded down, coating every inch of my husband's delicious Maztek cock.

CHAPTER 19

LAZ

Gabriella groaned, kicking off her covers in her sleep. I think she was dreaming about cupcakes. She draped one leg over the blanket, rolled over, and her grumbling snores resumed.

I had never been fond of the military-issued inflatable beds we used away from the main base. The twin-sized mattress never failed to do a number on my back, and sharing it with another person was even more painful than usual. But as I crossed the wavering tent to get a drink of water, I noticed that the numbing pain in my temples had disappeared.

Gabriella had given me the best sleep I had in years.

We could hear the faint pounding and drilling from the shuttle restoration crew through the slit of the tent opening. A trace of light was starting to spread through the black skies, hinting at dawn. I popped the cork out of my water bottle. As I drank, I looked at Gabriella again.

Gabriella was snoring louder than a drunken sailor, but she was the picture of serenity. Her hair fanned out across the pillow, and there was a hint of a smile on her face. As my eyes wandered across her exposed thigh and the curve of her ass peeking out from under the covers, I felt blood surge to my cock.

There was a good reason Gabriella was still out. We had been at it for three hours like we were the last people in the universe. I loved pussy of all colors, races, and creeds, but there was something about a tasty Earth woman that was sublime. All the restraint I had built up over the last few days had broken loose. Seeing Gabriella come out of her shell was refreshing. When she ordered me around and detailed how she wanted me to wreck her, it nearly drove me insane with desire.

"What time is it?" Gabriella moaned seductively and stretched her arms, pulling herself upright. She slid her leg back under the covers and covered her bare breasts.

"It's a quarter past four."

Gabriella smiled sleepily and fell back onto the pillow. "I don't think I've ever gotten up this early without wanting to smash my alarm clock. Go back to sleep. Aren't we leaving at five?"

"Yes, but there are still a few matters here that need my attention."

"I'm sure you have time to spare." Gabriella turned her lips down in a pout. She leaned back sultrily, pushing the covers down her body. She shook her body slightly, making her breasts bounce. Gabriella gently massaged the puffy bud of one of her nipples. "Why don't you kill some time here? I promise I'll make it worth your while."

My cock started growing as she slipped her finger between her lips. I imagined her sucking me off as her lovely blue eyes gave me a taste of what was to come. I took a deep breath and averted my eyes from the temptress. I was already running late.

"You know I want to, but I..." Something didn't sound right. I lost my train of thought and wondered what was bothering me.

"Laz?" Gabriella frowned. She sat up and leaned back against the wall. "Is something wrong?"

I turned toward the tent opening, listening intently. Nothing. That was the problem - there wasn't any noise. I heard a howling gust of wind blow past the entrance. Then there was nothing but silence. The sound of my men's drilling had stopped.

"Get dressed and wait here." Play time was over.

Gabriella stumbled out of the cot and slipped back into her jumpsuit. I pulled my shirt over my head. Sliding a gas mask over my face and grabbing a pair of binoculars, I headed outside to investigate.

Outside the tent, I saw the messy remnants of an after party. A breeze carried a hint of smoke from the warning fires coming from a pile of charred logs in the center of the camp. The inexperienced drinkers who couldn't hold their liquor lounged around the bonfire; some had drool coming out of their mouths. Everything appeared to be in order. The tents were undisturbed, with light, rhythmic breathing and an occasional cough coming from within.

Footsteps rustled on my right. Ganto, one of the crew technicians, stepped out from behind a thicket of dangling gray trees. He had red hair, which drew attention to the freckles on his pasty face. Ganto looked ill.

"Greetings, Ganto. What's the status on our shuttles?"

"General." Ganto rubbed the back of his neck. "My apologies – the stew from last night didn't agree with my stomach. I've been running back and forth for the past couple of hours. The last time I checked, the team was still working on the main shuttle's communication systems. We're in the process of getting a signal from Maztek, but there's something causing interference. We can't wrap our heads around it."

"How long will it take for you to figure it out?"

"I can't say for sure, General. I estimate another two hours at least."

I pointed the binoculars at the work site and peered into the eyepiece. The machinery was still operational. We had attached long hoses to the tanks, actively pumping fuel into the shuttles in preparation for the flight home. Half-loaded equipment and tool boxes stood next to a shuttle with an open compartment door. As I scanned the rest of the spaceships, I noticed something was missing.

"Why isn't the crew working?"

A glowing light lay on the dirt ground. My stomach lurched as I swept the scene. I finally saw them on the outskirts of our surroundings.

Someone had piled the bullet-ridden bodies of the entire crew behind a shuttle. They had concealed the corpses to pass a casual inspection. What happened to the guards? I shifted my binoculars to find that the young Maztek soldiers assigned to guard duty were out of commission.

"They must be working. Have you looked everywhere? We're running constant shifts."

"Ganto, I think we need to get down right now." I lowered my binoculars and dropped to the floor, reaching out to pull him to the ground. I was too late.

A steel bullet flew through the air, hitting Ganto straight in the forehead. I never knew what he was going to say to me. He died with words stuck in his throat. As indigo liquid trickled out of the circular hole in his forehead, he fell to his knees and hit the ground.

Even in death, Ganto would still assist his team. I reached out to grab the lakstar tusk from his belt, intended for only the direst emergencies. My cheeks swelled as I blew into the horn. The blaring call resonated throughout the campsite. "We're under attack! Protect the King!"

It was too early in the morning for most soldiers to be awake, but they roused themselves quickly, rubbing their eyes and getting their weapons ready. As some started to form defensive positions, and others made a dash for King Jacquim's tent, the Xylo forces revealed themselves. The distinct red and black colors appeared all around us.

We outmanned the small Xylo strike force, but we were unprepared and had foolishly spent the night celebrating. Those of us who still had booze in their systems were the first killed. Sniper shots caught them off-guard, sending them toppling to the ground.

Dallas' Herculean frame lumbered through the chaos, heading straight for the brides' quarters. I ducked back into my tent to arm myself.

"What's going on out there? It sounds like a war is happening right outside the door."

"Synic and her men found us." I pulled out my laser pistol, checking the charge and turning off the safety.

"Why would she do that? We captured most of her team already. Whatever misfits she scraped together aren't going to have a chance against your forces."

"Normally that would be true, but they have the element of surprise. But I think it's a suicide mission." I handed her a spare laser. "Stay here. Don't try anything stupid. If you ever think about listening to me, this would be the time to stay here and not go wandering off."

"I will." Gabriella nodded. She stood on the tips of her toes, wrapping her arms around my head and kissing me on the cheek. "Be careful."

Outside the tent, the world was a cacophony of blaze and gore. I felt calm and ready for battle. Distinct sounds called out to me, directing my shots as I fired laser blasts at the enemy.

Around me, soldiers took cover behind raised shields and carefully aimed their weapons. It had taken a few minutes, but the imminent danger had finally focused the men. A separate group of soldiers engaged the Xylo forces in hand-to-hand combat. King Jacquim fought in the thick of battle. He disarmed one of the Xylo, snatching his opponent's laser. After smashing the enemy in the head with the butt of the Xylo's weapon, he pulled out a knife and sliced it cleanly across his attacker's throat.

Three Xylo equipped with spears and lasers charged towards me. I managed to shoot two of them before they had time to pull their triggers. I lunged at the remaining guard, twisting the pike out of his slippery hands in one swift motion. As I gutted him with the long spear, his eyes swelled out of their sockets. I growled, driving the skewered Xylo into the trunk of a tree.

I started to look for the next enemy to engage, but an unseen force ripped my laser out of my hands. It sailed through the air, landing about a hundred feet away from me.

Synic stood at the foot of the hill, without a mask. She gathered her long black hair on one side of her neck, letting it flap in the blowing breeze. Her right hand was raised and the corners of her mouth curled in a thin-lipped, sinister smile.

I leaped toward my weapon, but I was thrown off my feet once again. It was difficult for me to think. I needed a weapon. Anything would do. I lunged for a dagger next to a stiff Xylo corpse. Even though it wasn't a throwing knife, I tested the weight and launched it at Synic. She dodged my clumsy attack, and the blade penetrated into the bark of a tree next to her.

Maybe I didn't need weapons. I made a fist and ran straight for the despot. Unprepared for my foolhardy assault, she let me spring on top of her and pin her hands. My hair knot collapsed when I collided with Synic and hung loosely over my face. Synic smelled horrible. The stench of rot leaked out of her mouth. When I positioned her cold wrists together to apply the restraints, she freed her legs and hooked her boots around my neck, forcing me off of her.

I flipped over in the air but managed to land on my hands and feet. As I started toward Synic, I felt my body slowly lifting off the ground. Synic's shoulders bounced as she snickered, her steady hands pantomiming an invisible choke-hold. It felt like someone had their hands wrapped around my neck. I was finding it difficult to breathe, and my vision was beginning to go dark.

For some reason, I still tried to speak. "You...you'll..."

"Save your breath, General." Synic turned out her bottom lip, batting her eyes at me. "You're pathetic. My parents said I wouldn't succeed in a man's world. I wish I hadn't cut out their tongues. If they could see me now, they would be able to tell me how wrong they were."

As I impotently brushed my throat, gurgles were the only thing that came out of my mouth.

"Any last words?"

While Synic was distracted talking to me, King Jacquim crept up behind her. He carried a large rock and bashed it against the side of her head. I plummeted to the ground, gasping as fresh air surged back into my lungs. The King crawled toward me, stretching out his hand.

I looked past the King and saw movement. Synic was slowly sitting up on the ground. A stream of blood was pouring down the side of her face.

She reached for a fallen rifle and aimed the barrel at us.

I didn't want it to be the King's time to die. "Get out of the way, sir!" I tried to leap to my feet, but I was too late.

Synic fired two shots. With an expression of peace on his face, King Jacquim slumped to the ground.

"No!"

The shriek came from Gabriella, who dashed out of the tent. She ran to King Jacquim, miraculously evading live fire as she dragged him inside. I felt numb as adrenaline took control of my body.

I yanked the dagger out of the tree branch. As Synic hysterically laughed, I pulled her off the floor. Pinning her up against the tree, I looked into her glossy black eyes, shoving the blade into her gut. I twisted it violently until I made sure I saw her struggling, short-winded breath fade into the wind.

I tossed the empty husk aside and raced back to my tent. Gabriella was on the ground with King Jacquim's head elevated on her lap. Her hands were wrapped around his when she looked up at me with teary eyes. She shook her head sadly.

"King Jacquim. Hold on. We're going to get you help."

"Don't bother." Even in his predicament, the King could laugh. "I'm aware there isn't much time left. You've got a good woman here."

"It's not over, my King."

"Stop. That is an order." His voice grew softer with every word, and his eyelids were taking longer and longer to open. "Promise me something, Laz."

I got down on one knee, bowing my head.

"Look after my beautiful planet, but most of all, take care of Ayala for me. With Synic's reign at an end, do everything you can to keep the peace."

"You have my word, King Jacquim."

"Good, good. Be kind to one another, naimas."

The King breathed out deeply, shutting his eyes for the last time.

CHAPTER 20

GABRIELLA, THREE WEEKS LATER

I leaned forward, laying a bouquet of white and blue poppies on the stairs in front of me. Taking a step back, I looked all the way up, admiring a ten-foot tall statue on a bronze pedestal. Talented Maztek sculptors had chiseled the majestic form from jade, and encapsulated Dad's likeness in exquisite detail. The statue depicted Dad wearing a lab coat. His initials were prominently displayed on the chest pocket. A pair of gold-rimmed frames fashioned from real gold sat on his nose. With one hand fixed on his hip, he gazed out into the distance, his grin set for eternity.

The park custodians were taking excellent care of the statue. The fifteen-year-old sculpture looked perfectly polished and the dazzling rays of the sun bounced off the surface.

When I first saw it, I thought it had been erected last week.

"Look at you, Dad. You look incredible."

Hiking up the flowing raven-black fabric of my dress, I dropped to my knees. I reached out to the silver-plated plaque, touching each word with my fingers. "In remembrance of Dr. Keith Marshall Hathaway – a brave soul with unmatched integrity, and a human who truly valued love and understanding above all. May he forever rest in peace."

"I miss you, Dad. Wherever you are. I wish you could see how much you've done for the Maztek, and how much you've done for me."

A tear rolled off my cheek, splashing against the year indicating my father's demise. It marked the end of a life cut short before its time.

"Excuse me. Are you all right?"

I wiped my cheeks hastily and turned around. A Maztek woman with a braided ponytail stood in front of me, carrying a basket of groceries in her arms. She set down her basket and approached me slowly.

"Don't mind me," I assured her with a tear-eyed smile. "I'm fine. I was just admiring the statue, that's all."

"Ah, yes. Dr. Hathaway. What a beautiful human." She touched the small pendant around her neck, twirling the tiny pink gem pensively. "Are you his daughter?"

"I am. How did you know?"

"We all know. You have Marshall's eyes. I could recognize them anywhere." The woman's lip trembled as she lowered her hand to her chest. "He's not dead, you know. He lives through you."

"You know something? All my life, no one ever mentioned my Dad on Earth. But now that I'm on a different planet, that's all I ever hear from anyone. It's bizarre."

"Maybe so, but you'll get accustomed to it. Your father touched all our lives – some more than others."

"Did you know him, too?"

"Not personally." The woman's voice was filled with emotion. "We were strangers. That made what he did for me incredible."

"Why do you say that?"

"At the time, I was fifteen, and eight months pregnant. The father of my child had abandoned me the moment I informed him of the pregnancy, so he was no longer in the picture. Both my parents had perished in the Fallgold incident and I was living on the streets. My baby decided she wanted to come out earlier than expected. I was bleeding and couldn't understand why. Every doctor turned me away when they found out I was poor – everyone except Dr. Hathaway."

The woman paused for a moment, lost in thought.

"If I had run into your father only thirty minutes later, I would have lost my baby. Dr. Hathaway did not specialize in deliveries, but he called in some favors and a team appeared like magic. Four harrowing hours later, she was born."

"That's absolutely beautiful," I whispered. My heart swelled with so much pride that it threatened to burst from my chest. "It sounds like something Dad would have done. I'm glad to hear your baby made it."

"She's not a baby any longer." The woman pointed out a young girl with a short, spiky haircut, sitting by the stream. The teenager picked flowers from the grass and took apart the petals, making small homes for the insects. "She's the reason I wake up every morning. Her name is Marleigh. I named her after the kind doctor who helped bring her to this world."

"That's a pretty name. I..."

"Gabriella?"

Cheyenne ambled up the path from my left, dressed in black robes similar to mine.

"Come on. It's starting."

"I have to go." I smiled at the woman one more time, touching her gently on the arm. "Thank you."

* * * *

A somber mass of thousands of Maztek bodies left no spaces in the bleachers around me. The breathtaking circular dome of the Fallgold Colosseum was packed, but the air was supernaturally quiet. It seemed like everyone was holding a glowing candle, brightly illuminating the dome. Garlands of flowers weaved in and out of the pillars. Gold and white tapered candlesticks hovered over the triangular center stage. The ceiling of the dome displayed a moving image of diamond stars on a mystical violet night background.

"...Specialist Artillery Gunner Maxwell Radley, Specialist Sniper Scout Jarrod Woodacre, and last, but not least – my father, Jacquim."

I stopped looking around the dome and focused on the stage. The tiny figure of Princess Ayala dipped its head forward, her white-blonde locks of hair cascading around her shoulders and shielding her face. She removed her crown, holding the circle of intricate gold thorns encrusted with pearls and precious stones over her heart. I spotted Laz, Dallas, and Kraig in the front row. Their chests glinted with arrays of shiny medals and pins. They too bowed their heads for a moment of silence.

Princess Ayala turned to the podium next to her and raised a silver champagne flute. "Tonight is a memorial to the dead. We give unending thanks to our military for bringing the hostages home safe and sound, as well as finally defeating the Xylox oppression. We remember the fallen souls for their bravery and for playing a crucial role in restoring peace and sovereignty to Maztek. May their memories live on forever, and may their legacies continue. Malam gambi."

"Malam gambi."

Voices echoed throughout the dome in unison. Simultaneously, we blew out our candles, enveloping the room in a solemn darkness. The lights in the Colosseum slowly flickered back to life.

As I started to make my way down the bleachers, Cheyenne rose from her seat next to me. "Gabriella." She tugged on my wrist. "Princess Ayala would like to see you."

"Me?" I raised an eyebrow. "What, like right now?"

"No time like the present," Cheyenne said enthusiastically, nudging me down the steps of the bleachers.

"Alright, alright – I'm going!"

As we reached the landing, Cheyenne flashed me a giddy wink before disappearing into the crowd. I waited by the foot of the stage. I wasn't going to burst in on alien royalty. Princess Ayala had her back to me. She was speaking to a group of kingdom attendants. One of them motioned to her, and the Princess stopped abruptly.

"Wonderful. She is here." She clapped her hands together and gestured at me. "Come on, ladies, there is no time to waste!"

That was the last thing I remember hearing before a mob of servants closed in around me. Two women slipped their arms around mine. They led me to a place I had only seen in passing: the back rooms of the dome. The princess walked smoothly down the stairs next to us.

The attendants led me behind a thick black curtain, pushing me into one of the dressing rooms. Before I knew it, two women were undoing the ribbons tied around my shoulders. As they pulled my black dress over my head, an attendant appeared at my side. She held a white gown which reached to the floor and had a lace, gold-accented train behind it. There were accessories, too. Rose pearls adorned the belt and shoulders of the draped Grecian sleeves.

"Is this for me?" My eyebrows shot up my forehead in disbelief. I wasn't in control of anything. The attendants slipped the gown over my head, smoothing it over my body. I spun around in a circle, gazing at the mirror which appeared front of me. The dress fit like a dream. The attendants behind me began combing out my hair. The ones in front of me attacked my face with powder puffs and sparkly makeup. "Why am I getting the Princess treatment?"

"I know you were the last person my father saw before he died." Princess Ayala placed a hand over mine, gently squeezing. "Thank you for not leaving him to die alone."

"Of course. Anyone would have done the same thing."

As soon as the attendants finished fussing over me, Princess Ayala took me by the hand. She guided me out the dressing room and walked me toward the back doors of the Colosseum. The doors opened with a wave of her hand, allowing a radiant splash of afternoon sunlight to spill into the room. Princess Ayala took a colorful bundle of orchids, roses, and daisies from her attendant. She handed it to me with a smile.

"That's not true. Many would have run away. This is my way of saying thank you. You never had the chance to have an official wedding."

With shaking fingers holding on to the bouquet, I stepped out of the dome.

220

"Oh my God."

I stood on a white silk carpet rolled out over the lush grass. The carpet was sprinkled with flower petals, leading to a gorgeous floral arch at the end of the path. A lump started forming in my throat when I saw who was underneath the arch.

Laz stood waiting for me, wearing his finest set of Maztek army fatigues. Stylists had trimmed and carefully groomed his hair. His beard had been snipped and carefully groomed. I loved seen a clean alien in a uniform.

There were many people around us making noise, but I scanned them looking for one in particular. I found her in an instant. Cheyenne was sitting in the front row, and her cheers were the loudest of all. She sat next to Dallas and their arms were intertwined. She dropped his arm to wave at me enthusiastically.

I never thought I would have so many people cheering at my wedding.

As I started down the carpet, the orchestra next to the arch began to play a familiar melody. To my surprise, it wasn't the traditional wedding tune. A tear fell out of the corner of my eye, tainting the powdered blush on my cheeks.

The music I heard was Dad's lullaby.

It felt like my feet were floating down the aisle as I made my way toward Laz. Princess Ayala appeared behind the arch holding a rod of blessing. I couldn't stop smiling, and neither could Laz. He reached into his chest pocket, pulling out a gold band between his fingers. Precious Maztek stones adorned the circle of gold, and the diamond from my missing earring featured prominently in the center.

Laz slid the ring over my finger, leaning over to whisper something into my ear. "You look beautiful, naima."

I reached up and put both hands on his chin, pulling him in for a long, deep kiss.

"I'm forever yours, naima."

As I pulled away from Laz, Princess Ayala stepped between us.

"Brothers and sisters, we are gathered here today to celebrate the love and beauty of these two souls, and join them together for eternity."

If you enjoyed this book, please review it on Amazon. Your review helps me succeed as an author.

To stay up-to-date on my latest releases, sign up for my newsletter at:

http://lisalace.com/newsletter/

OTHER BOOKS BY LISA LACE

WATER WORLD WARRIOR: A TerraMates Novel

Why would I want to be married to an alien?

I should not have applied to TerraMates! The idea was crazy. I'm a young woman, in the prime of my life.

But I was desperate.

When I landed on another world, his appearance intrigued me. He dripped sexuality and moved like an animal. We have three days together before he sets sail without me. Am I going to escape or submit to my desires?

TAKEN: A TerraMates Novel

What happens when TerraMates runs out of applicants?

There's never a shortage of wealthy alien bachelors looking for the thrill of mating with a human. They want our women.

But despite the promise of riches, sometimes the pool of available brides runs dry.

How does TerraMates find more girls, and where do they go? When Lyzette gets taken off the street, she finds out.

WATER WORLD CONFIDENTIAL: A TERRAMATES NOVEL

He needed a wife. I wanted an alien lover.

The first time I saw Jori, I hated everything about him. He didn't care about anything except himself. On the other hand, his body was spectacular, and his muscles were firm. I couldn't stop thinking about him.

When TerraMates gave me the chance to marry Jori, I took it. I knew I needed the money. What I didn't know was that Jori's exterior was a facade, and he had kept secrets from everyone his entire life.

ALPHA'S ENSLAVED BRIDE: A TERRAMATES NOVEL

Knowing the future isn't a blessing. It's a curse. Especially when you've seen your death.

I'm going to die in the arms of someone I have never seen before. He's a person I will love, but I don't know anything about him.

When TerraMates matched me with Airik, I couldn't believe it. This sexy alien could see the future, just like me. I wasn't alone anymore. I quickly found out he knows nothing about Earth or humans. I married him, but will I be safe with him?

I didn't foresee I would want to feel his hands on my body.

I've never been able to change the future before. For us to survive, I need to.

AUCTIONED TO THE ALPHA: A TERRAMATES NOVEL

The innovative TerraMates business has been a runaway success. Who wouldn't want to marry an alien?

Seeking to expand, TerraMates has opened new locations with different business models.

Eden is looking for a fresh start and is one of the first mail-order brides from New York City. As soon as she signs the paperwork and collects her credits, she blacks out.

When Eden wakes up, she's been married to an alien bounty hunter. She's ready for a new beginning, but all she knows about her alien husband is that he's handsome and dangerous. Eden never dreamed she'd be chasing criminals through space!

WRONG ALIEN: A TERRAMATES NOVEL

Life isn't worth living without an Internet connection. I'm always on the computer, video chatting, and even reading books on my phone.

It was natural for me to use the TerraMates app to find a husband.

I didn't know they would match me with a sexy alien who was afraid of high technology and send me to a mysterious planet where the penalty for having a smartphone was execution!

CAPTURED BY THE ALIEN KING

When I saw my chance to get off Earth, I took it. I knew I needed to escape.

I didn't know I'd be claimed by an alien monarch in the middle of his mating season! Now we're on the run together, facing terrorists and natural disasters.

I'm still trying to figure out my feelings for this sexy guy. He is totally into me, but he has some unique ideas about alien romance...

www.ingramcontent.com/pod-product-compliance
Lightning Source LLC
Chambersburg PA
CBHW020610180626
46810CB00007B/2721